She woke, _____ ng disoriented

Her body was _____ xual release—a sens_____ d in a long time. In the dark she felt her face heat as wisps of the erotic dream of Andre drifted through her mind.

Something had snapped her out of the dream. A sound. It filtered into her consciousness, making the hairs on the back of her neck stand up and tingle. It was a woman's voice, chanting to the beat of a dream. Out in the humid night.

Morgan strained her ears, trying to figure out the words. But she couldn't make sense of them, and finally she concluded that they were in some language she didn't understand. An ancient language that sounded rough and primitive and…

She shivered. Evil. Yes, the chant sounded like pure evil.

SPELLBOUND

USA TODAY Bestselling Author

REBECCA YORK

RUTH GLICK WRITING AS REBECCA YORK

TORONTO • NEW YORK • LONDON
AMSTERDAM • PARIS • SYDNEY • HAMBURG
STOCKHOLM • ATHENS • TOKYO • MILAN • MADRID
PRAGUE • WARSAW • BUDAPEST • AUCKLAND

ISBN 0-373-22828-7

SPELLBOUND

Copyright © 2005 Ruth Glick

This edition published by arrangement with Harlequin Books S.A.

www.eHarlequin.com

Printed in U.S.A.

ABOUT THE AUTHOR

Award-winning, bestselling novelist Ruth Glick, who writes as Rebecca York, is the author of close to eighty books, including her popular 43 Light Street series for Harlequin Intrigue. Ruth says she has the best job in the world. Not only does she get paid for telling stories; she's also the author of twelve cookbooks. Ruth and her husband, Norman, travel frequently, researching locales for her novels and searching out new dishes for her cookbooks.

Books by Rebecca York

CAST OF CHARACTERS

Andre Gascon—Why did he live on an isolated estate in the bayou?

Morgan Kirkland—Had she come to Belle Vista to do a job—or had powerful forces summon her?

Linette Sonnier—Was she a figment of Morgan's imagination?

Yvonne Sonnier—Why did the voodoo priestess wish Andre ill?

Janet Laveren—Was she Morgan's friend or enemy?

Marlon Jarvis—Did he want to solve a difficult case—or obstruct justice?

Dwight Rivers—Did he resent Andre or wish him well?

Bubba Arnette—Did he disable Morgan's car?

Bob Mansard—Was his intention to solve the bayou murders or make trouble for Andre?

Rick Brevard—Did he have reasons to fear Andre?

Chapter One

The moment she asked the way to Belle Vista, Morgan Kirkland knew she was in trouble.

The gas station attendant stiffened, and the good ol' boys who had been lounging on a bench next to the soda machine came to attention.

"Belle Vista? Why do you need to know the way to that place?" the guy in the greasy overalls demanded.

She wanted to tell him in a steel-edged voice that her reasons were none of his business. But since the Light Street Detective Agency had sent her here on an undercover assignment, she gave him a tentative smile.

The patch on his right front pocket said his name was Bubba. She'd read all about him in the notes her client, Andre Gascon, had sent to Baltimore. Bubba Arnette was a high school dropout who pumped gas during the day. When the sun went down, he illegally trapped alligators in the bayou.

Trying to sound friendly, she spouted her cover story. "Mr. Gascon has hired me to catalog the books in his library with a view to possibly selling off some of the collection."

"Oh, yeah? You a librarian?" he challenged, staring

at her with the smug eyes of a man who thinks that any guy is the superior of any female.

She looked up at him through the car window, picturing what he saw: a very nonthreatening individual; a woman with straight, chin-length blond hair, blue eyes and a slender frame draped in a conservative beige skirt and a persimmon-colored blouse.

What he couldn't see was the martial arts training, the marksmanship badges, the woman who had abandoned caution along with cream in her coffee.

Really, she'd like to meet this guy in a dark alley and teach him some manners.

She took in a breath of the hot, humid air and let it out before answering, "Yes, I'm a librarian." She might not have a degree in the field, but she'd just been through an intensive crash course. The consultants from Baltimore's famous Pratt Library had pronounced her fit to decide whether to go with the Dewey Decimal System or Library of Congress cataloging.

"Well, you don't want to work for a secretive bastard like Gascon. He's bad news," the local expert allowed.

"In what way?"

"You want to get murdered, you drive right up to his estate, *chère.*"

Morgan gave him a wide-eyed look. In a shaky voice, she asked, "Murdered?"

"Guys end up in the bayou out by his place. Facedown in the muck. Clawed by a jaguar," he answered, a nasty ring to his voice. Apparently he was enjoying telling horror stories to the little librarian.

"There's a jaguar in the swamp?" she asked in a quavering tone, pretending he'd had the desired effect, wishing she were free to wipe the smug smile off his weaselly face.

One of the good ol' boys, a guy in his fifties with thinning hair combed across his bald pate and an inner-tube belly hiding his belt, pushed himself off the bench and ambled over to join the conversation.

"Bubba here is just giving you some friendly advice." He fixed her with a piercing look. "My cousin Willie shoulda listened to him. Leastways if he didn't want to croak hisself."

"Thank you all for the warnings," she answered. "But Mr. Gascon has already given me a retainer. I need the money, and I'm not about to return it."

"Suit yourself, *chère*," Rubber Belly said. Probably he was Bob Mansard, cousin of Willie Mansard, who had indeed ended up clawed to death in the swamp. Until his demise, Willie had been one of the troublemakers in town. Bob seemed to be ripped from the same cloth.

Gascon had told her about the local men and about the cat legend. He'd characterized the guys in humorous terms. She'd gotten the "rubber belly" description from him. But he'd never joked about the big cat. He'd said the murderer was a man—a man wearing claws. And he had hired her to find out who it was.

Thinking she'd like to cut the chitchat short—and use the facilities before arriving at Belle Vista—she asked, "Is the ladies' room locked?"

"Key's right there," Bubba answered, pointing to a hook inside the door of the station.

With all eyes on her, Morgan resisted the urge to focus on her beige sandals as she walked past the on-lookers, retrieved the key, then hurried around the side of the building.

The rest room wasn't a place where she wanted to stay very long, so she was in and out as quickly as she could manage.

When she returned, a couple of the guys in the peanut gallery seemed to be enjoying some kind of joke, and she had the feeling they'd been talking about the new Belle Vista librarian while she'd been gone. She wanted to whirl and ask what was so funny, but that would have been out of character. So she paid for her gas, climbed back into her rental car and drove farther into town.

Over the past few weeks, her new client had e-mailed her a great deal of material about the area, the local residents and his own estate. She'd wondered if his assessment was too harsh, but now that she was in town, it was easy to see what he'd been talking about. These guys didn't like him. More than that, it sounded as if they were holding him personally responsible for anything bad that happened in the backcountry.

She got a better impression of St. Germaine, population ten thousand, when she reached the restored business area. Two blocks of charming, old brick and stucco two-story buildings had been scrubbed and painted into what Gascon had called "a tourist-trap shopping delight." Although she found a hardware store and a small grocery, the majority of the businesses were antique shops, art galleries, T-shirt "factories," a handicraft co-op and restaurants.

The town was definitely open for business, but the free parking lot next to the grocery store was only a third full on a Friday afternoon. And all of the retail businesses lining the brick sidewalks featured prominent Sale signs in the windows. Beyond the shops was a two-story Victorian that housed the chamber of commerce.

After pulling up next to a well-kept Cadillac, Morgan went inside.

The woman behind the counter glanced up immediately. "Can I help you?" she inquired, as though speaking to her new best friend.

Morgan thought she was probably Sadie Delay, since she fit the description Gascon had given her of one of the women who worked in the office.

"I'm just looking," Morgan answered. As she began picking up some of the brochures for bayou boat rides and outlet malls fifty miles away, a tall, well-built man bustled out of the back office.

"Dwight Rivers, president of the chamber of commerce," he said in a hearty, booming voice that Gascon had described as a bullhorn in search of a crowd to control. "What can we do to help you? Are you vacationing in the area?"

"I might," she said because she didn't want to get into the kind of hostile situation she'd created at the gas station.

The man stuck out a broad hand, which she felt compelled to shake.

Cautiously she tried a testing remark. "I would have expected to see more people around town on a Friday afternoon."

He sighed. "So would I."

"Is there some problem in town?"

"Just the slow season."

Right. For the past eight months.

"The guys at the gas station told me that there had been some deaths in the swamp."

His features darkened. "Well, they talk too much."

"Sorry, I'm just trying to—"

"No, that's okay. It's not your fault. I understand why you'd be nervous. There's talk of a big cat prowling the bayou country, and that's hurt business here. But you're perfectly safe in town. In fact, we have several charming bed-and-breakfast establishments that would love to have you stay with them. I can call one of the owners for you right now."

"I'll have to think about it," she answered quickly. Before he could push any more of the town's attractions on her, she turned and walked out the door. Probably in the next few hours he'd hear through the grapevine that she was working for Gascon. Maybe he'd think she'd been less than honest with him. But she could always use the gas station as an excuse. Who would want to get into two confrontations in the space of half an hour if she could avoid them?

She lingered in town for perhaps fifteen minutes, taking a self-guided tour, noting the wide lawns and old mansions in the better areas and the smaller, ramshackle houses with faded paint and missing siding on the metaphorical wrong side of the tracks.

Swinging back onto Main Street, she headed for the road that she knew would take her to Belle Vista. Gascon had asked her to arrive before dark. Although she still had plenty of time, she couldn't help feeling a sense of urgency now.

The last dwelling inside the town limits was a two-story farmhouse. Though the gray siding needed painting, the lawn and shrubbery were well kept. But it wasn't the landscaping that caught Morgan's attention. The window to the right of the green-painted front door sported a sign that made her eyes widen.

It said: Voodoo Priestess.

Morgan, whose sensibilities were firmly planted in the culture of the north, had always thought of voodoo as an ancient cult—and one that was never quite respectable. Apparently in St. Germaine it was okay to advertise yourself as a priestess right out in the open.

Why hadn't Gascon mentioned it in all the information he'd given her about the area? Was it an oversight—or a deliberate omission?

She'd slowed down to look at the house and the sign. As she stared at the window, a hand pulled the curtain aside, revealing a woman with a creamy complexion and long, shiny hair as dark as midnight. When the woman's dark gaze zeroed in on her, Morgan felt something like a physical blow to the center of her chest. For a moment she couldn't move, couldn't breathe. Then her foot bounced on the accelerator, and she jerked forward, before deliberately smoothing out her speed.

What was that?

Her own out-of-kilter reaction, or something emanating from the woman?

Had the priestess somehow known she was coming to town? Had Gascon told her? Or had she seen Morgan in her crystal ball?

No, that was the wrong image. Probably a voodoo priestess would be looking at chicken entrails.

Morgan snorted. *You're just letting this place spook you. The way nothing has spooked you in recent memory.*

Stepping on the gas, she sped up, glad to leave the cheery little community behind. St. Germaine had certainly darkened her mood. As if to reinforce the oppressive feeling, she could see storm clouds gathering. Now they were purple edged, like a giant bruise covering the sky.

A battered green pickup truck was behind her. When she turned onto the narrow road that would take her to Belle Vista, the other driver did the same. Looking in the rearview mirror, she tried to see who was back there.

Two men, as far as she could tell, both wearing baseball caps pulled down over their eyes.

The truck stayed on her tail, a constant presence, making her feel as if she was being stalked. She slowed down, hoping whoever it was would pass. But the car kept matching its speed with hers.

She was in isolated country now, the road an intrusion in the green-and-brown landscape. Stretches of dark water, gnarled pines and low palmettos crowded the shoulders. Cypresses loomed in the distance.

Andre Gascon had described this countryside to her in his e-mails. He'd made it sound beautiful and poetic. A vast area lush with vegetation that was a perfect natural habitat for birds and animals. But now that she was out here alone with a pickup too close behind her, she wished for some signs of civilization.

She hadn't seen a house in miles. And the vultures circling overhead weren't exactly reassuring.

The wind flared, whipping at the Spanish moss hanging from the branches of the taller trees, and a few fat drops of rain landed on the windshield.

When she spotted a sign that said, Warning, Flash Flood Area, she muttered, "Oh great!"

The truck sped up, crowding too close, and she thought the driver would finally pass. Instead he started riding her bumper, making her wonder if he was drunk.

Increasing her speed, she tried to get away, then took a curve too fast and realized she'd better slow down. When she pressed on the brake, though, the response was sluggish, the mechanism no longer working correctly.

The road was narrow, and as she turned the next corner, she wove into the wrong lane. Thankful that there was no traffic coming the other way, she yanked herself back onto the right side of the blacktop as she frantically pumped the brake pedal. Despite her best efforts, the car hurtled forward.

The blacktop had quite a few bends now. Her hands melded in a death grip on the wheel as she struggled to keep from shooting off the paved surface.

Then she hit a sharp turn and found herself sailing off the wrong side of the road, onto the shoulder. Gravel crunched under her wheels, slowing her somewhat. But it was already too late to retain control of the car. One tire plunged downward, and she plowed into a water-filled ditch.

Mud sucked at her tires, and to her relief, the car rocked to a halt. The sudden stop carried her forward, but the seat belt snapped her back into place again.

She sat behind the wheel, slightly dazed, trying to catch her breath as she took inventory. As far as she could tell, she was okay. The engine was still running, so she cut it off, feeling the vehicle shudder and go still.

The accident hadn't been her fault. Her brakes had failed, and only the ditch had prevented her from tearing off into the swamp.

The car had been okay on the highway from New Orleans. And it had still been fine when she'd toured St. Germaine forty minutes ago.

Now her brakes were shot. Had Bubba done something to them while she'd been in the ladies' room? Was that the big joke the guys had been laughing about?

Or was it the voodoo priestess who had hexed her car on the way out of town?

That last thought made hysterical laughter bubble up in her throat. It choked off quickly when she caught a flash of movement in the side mirror. The pickup truck that had followed her from town had stopped a little way down the shoulder. As she watched, two guys wearing baseball caps got out.

After a brief conversation, they started walking toward her. Did they intend to help a lady in distress? Or were they planning to have some fun—or worse—with the librarian stranded on an isolated road in the bayou?

One of them was tall and muscular. The other was short and squat, with a big belly. It could be Bob Mansard, although she couldn't tell for sure because his face was hidden by his baseball cap and sunglasses.

Maybe good old Bob had made the suggestion about messing with her vehicle. Maybe Bubba had put a pinhole leak in the brake-fluid line, so that the car would drive normally until she was well out of town.

And maybe not. Still, she wasn't going to take a chance on the goodwill of these guys.

Quickly she ducked down below the dashboard, retrieving the purse that had fallen on the floor of the passenger side.

Unwilling to wait in the car like a sitting duck, she pulled out her Glock and gripped it in her free hand as she opened the car door. It hit against the edge of the ditch, and a green lizard scurried out of the way. The creature drew her gaze to the dark, scummy water, and she felt her stomach knot as she thought of what else lived in its depths. At least the position of the car meant she could leap to the shoulder without getting wet.

Scrambling out into the hot, heavy air, she faced the men, holding the gun down along her leg where they couldn't see it. They ambled toward her as if they owned this deserted stretch of road and their quarry was completely at their mercy.

Well, they were in for a big surprise. Back at the gas station, she hadn't wanted to reveal her real purpose in coming to St. Germaine. But she could take these guys, just the way she could take anybody else who had dared to mess with her over the past two years.

She thrived on danger, and now she could feel adrenaline pumping through her veins.

"Bring it on," she muttered under her breath.

She was about to raise the gun and shout, "Hold it right there," when they both stopped short, as if they'd gotten a subliminal jolt of her thoughts.

One of them made a strangled sound, and she allowed herself a moment of satisfaction.

Then she saw that neither one of them was looking in her direction at all. They were staring toward the bayou, toward the darker shade under a stand of pines.

About thirty feet away was a large cat.

A jaguar, she thought. The jaguar Andre Gascon had convinced her was simply a local myth that someone was using to cause trouble between him and the town of St. Germaine. But this animal was no figment of her imagination. And his glowing yellow eyes were trained right on her.

Chapter Two

In the background Morgan heard the sound of feet running, doors slamming, an engine roaring to life.

Tires spun on gravel as the truck in back of her made a U-turn and sped away, leaving her alone on the shoulder of the road—staring into the golden eyes of the jaguar.

Details assaulted her. The animal looked to be about two hundred pounds of spotted, muscular body, with huge paws and a black-tipped muzzle.

Once Andre Gascon had mentioned the jaguar myth, she'd researched the animals, because she was always thorough in her preparations for an assignment. She knew that the cats were most common in Central America, but they also inhabited the southern United States. Still, no matter where they lived, the stealthy creatures were seldom seen during the day—or at all.

As she stood facing the cat, all the stories she'd read about local residents mauled in the bayou and left for dead came to mind.

With a start, she realized that the gun was still dangling beside her leg. She raised the weapon now, taking it in a two-handed grip as she faced the animal.

One thing she knew, if the cat was responsible for the deaths in the bayou, she wasn't going to be his next victim.

She thought that with one part of her brain. With another part, she decided that the animal looked too regal to be a man killer. She didn't know how she came to that conclusion. She only knew that laying the blame for the bayou killings on the shoulders of this beast felt wrong.

Drops of rain began to trickle onto her head and shoulders as she stood on the shoulder of the road, still as a statue, facing the jaguar. For several moments, he continued to regard her with that unnerving intelligence. She didn't know what she would have done if he had come any closer. Maybe fired a warning shot into the air.

But she didn't have to put her nerves to the test because the animal took a step back, then another, moving slowly as though he knew that spooking a woman with an automatic pistol was a bad idea.

When the jaguar had backed away several paces, he turned and flipped his tail at her like an annoyed house cat. Then, with a mighty leap, he took off, racing away into the darkness under the trees.

She blinked and breathed out a sigh, wondering if the whole incident had been a fantasy. Then she reminded herself that she hadn't been the only one to see the cat. The men in the baseball caps had taken off like frightened weasels.

Lowering the gun, she looked up and down the narrow ribbon of blacktop. The cat had come to her rescue as if he'd known she was in trouble from the men. But now she had another problem. She was stranded out here. The whole time she'd been on this road, she hadn't seen another vehicle, except the truck that had been following her.

Earlier, there had been no point in calling 911. By the time help arrived, the men would have done whatever they'd planned.

Now the situation was different. Climbing back into the car, she set the gun on the passenger seat and pulled her cell phone from her purse. But when she tried to make a call, she couldn't get a connection. Either this part of Louisiana was too isolated, or the storm was interfering.

As if to bolster the latter theory, a bolt of lightning flashed in front of her. Several seconds later thunder rumbled.

So now what? The car's brakes were weak. If she had another choice, she wouldn't drive. But staying here was dangerous, since the guys in the truck could come back after they figured the big cat was gone.

She wasn't the kind of person who could sit still waiting for trouble. She had to *do* something and she figured that waiting here was more dangerous than trying to drive. Hopefully, she could make it to Belle Vista, then arrange to have the car towed to another gas station. Or maybe even to another town.

ANDRE GASCON came running through the rain from the field behind his house. He made a dash for his car, dove behind the wheel and started the engine, stomped on the accelerator, then skidded down the driveway.

Janet had heard from a friend in town that Morgan had stopped in St. Germaine for gas. Probably she'd let on where she was going, which was a big mistake. He wouldn't put it past Bubba Arnette or one of his buddies to do something to her car.

Andre clenched his fists and cursed. He'd asked her to drive straight through from New Orleans. But he hadn't insisted, because he hadn't wanted to creep her out before she even got here.

If anyone had asked him how he knew she was in trouble now, he would have put it down to intuition.

But that was a lie. He *knew.*

And in truth, he'd been waiting for something bad to happen since this morning.

The sky looked like the inside of a coal mine. It wasn't because night was coming. He still had time before sunset. The darkness came from the storm clouds hanging heavy over the bayou.

A few drops hit the windshield, like fingers tapping against the glass, a ghostly presence begging admittance.

His stomach had long ago tied itself in knots.

He'd snapped awake at seven that morning, after an almost sleepless night, prepared to hear a phone call telling him that she'd changed her mind and was taking an assignment at the South Pole instead. But she hadn't made the call.

Relief had been like a cool breeze blowing on his feverish skin. Still, he'd kept picking up the phone and putting it down. Finally he'd checked in with her office on the pretext that he wanted to make sure of her arrival schedule. In truth, her itinerary had been engraved on his memory since she'd e-mailed it to him.

Her plane had landed three hours ago. She should have been here by now. Instead he pictured her sitting in her car in the middle of the flash flood area.

The image turned him cold all over as he sped down the plantation road and onto the highway, his hands gripping the wheel so hard his knuckles turned white.

MORGAN KNEW she was in trouble. The rain had picked up, restricting her vision. But when she opened the car door a crack, she could see that the sides of the ditch were even slicker than before. Her lips set in a grim line, she tried to back up, then rock the car forward and onto the road. After several repetitions, all she succeeded in doing was making the tires sink deeper into the mud.

"Damn!" It was raining harder now. She wanted to huddle inside the car and keep dry, but she knew the longer the vehicle stayed in the ditch, the less likely she was to get it out. Maybe she could put something under the wheels.

Rolling down the side window, she spotted a big patch of spiky ferns. They were worth a try. She scrambled out, this time slipping in the mud and almost dropping her gun.

Tucking it in the waistband of her skirt, she walked down the road toward the ferns, sheets of rain pounding her now.

She'd gotten a dozen yards from the car when she heard a roaring noise. Not the jaguar. Something much louder and more ominous. The sound was nothing like the one an animal would make. Instead she knew she was listening to an elemental force of nature bearing down on her.

Her head jerked up, and she looked in all directions. She couldn't see the danger. Not yet. But she turned and started running back to the relative safety of the vehicle.

She had taken only a few steps when a wall of something plowed through the trees on the other side of the road.

It was a dark wave of water, sweeping away everything in its path, catching Morgan in its cold embrace.

With the force of a tornado, it lifted her feet off the ground. A scream tore from her throat as the current spun her around like a plastic doll and flung her into the bayou.

She screamed again as the water carried her farther from the road. She was a good swimmer, but it was impossible to do more than keep her head above the surface.

Things whipped past her. A black snake. A plastic milk jug. A clump of vegetation. Her jacket, shoes and skirt were torn from her body as though someone had rudely yanked them away.

When she felt her shoulder hit something, her arms shot up and clamped on. It was a young tree, bowing under the force of the water.

Desperately she clung to the trunk, even as the water tried to tear her away and send her to join the clothing that had disappeared downstream.

Rain pelted her head, and the roar of the roiling water pounded her ears. She was scared. And that was a novelty.

For the past two years—since Trevor had died in an ambush in Afghanistan—she'd been afraid of nothing and no one. She'd walked into dangerous situations like someone else would walk into a bedroom. She'd disarmed men twice her size. She'd chased a fugitive across the roofs of Baltimore town houses, jumping a five-foot gap three stories above the ground.

She'd thought she didn't care what happened to her. Yet now she fought the deluge that tried to sweep her away, inching into a better position so that the tree trunk partially shielded her from the worst of the current. As she clasped the slippery bark, she knew that something within herself had changed. She didn't want to die.

Not here. Not like this.

ANDRE SCREECHED his SUV to a halt, taking in the scene in a split second. A torrent of water poured across the road, and Morgan's car was stuck in a ditch on the other side. Unless she was below the dashboard for some reason, she wasn't in the car.

Merde!

Fear was a vise, squeezing the breath out of his lungs. He wanted to rage in agony and anger. Instead he cupped his hands around his mouth and called her name as he scanned the bayou and the water. "Morgan!"

When he spotted a splash of persimmon color out in the water, his heart lurched inside his chest. The blob of color resolved itself into fabric. Her blouse, half-open. As the frightening picture came into focus, he saw the graceful column of her neck and her short blond hair. She was in profile to him, clinging desperately to a slender tree trunk as the water tore at her.

"Morgan, hang on," he called. "I'm coming. Just hang on."

If she heard him, she didn't answer above the roar of the water.

He focused on keeping his mind working rationally as he ran back to his vehicle and grabbed the rope that was part of his emergency kit. First he thought he could throw it to her, then he canceled that idea. She might be partially sheltered by the tree trunk, but letting go of it to grab the lifeline would be too dangerous.

Instead he tied one end of the rope to a nearby tree. After testing it, he tied the other end around his waist and waded into the water. Immediately, the current gave a vicious tug on his body, trying to drag him away. But he gritted his teeth and kept his footing.

"Hang on," he called again as he struggled toward Morgan.

OVER THE SOUND of the raging elements, Morgan thought she heard someone calling to her.

There was only one person who knew her name—who had been expecting her.

Hoping against hope, she called out, "Mr. Gascon?"

"Yes," he answered, his deep voice carrying above the roar of the water.

"Thank God."

"I'm coming."

He was closer now, in the water, but she dared not twist herself around to look at him.

"I think under the circumstances, you can call me Andre." He said it with a wry note in his voice between puffs of breath.

He must be strong. Strong enough to waste his breath on talking.

"You're doing great. Fantastic. I'm almost there."

She clung to the sound of his words, and he kept talking to her, his voice strong and reassuring over the raging water as he told her that everything was going to be all right. In just a few more moments he would pull her to safety.

Centuries passed before she felt a hard, male body press against her back, cupping itself protectively around her.

She let out a deep sigh of relief when his form blocked the worst of the raging water.

He held her tightly, his cheek against the top of her head, as though his relief at making contact was as great as hers.

"Thank the Lord," he whispered.

"Yes."

"I'll get you to shore. But don't let go yet," he cautioned.

He moved behind her, doing something she couldn't see. Then a rope slipped over her head and shoulders.

"Loosen one hand," he ordered as he held her in place.

She released her death grip on the tree, feeling the tug of the water. But he shielded her as he worked the rope farther down her body.

"Good. That's good. Now turn around. Then I'll turn so we're facing back toward the shore."

The water buffeted them as he turned her in his arms, clasping her to himself like a lover, as though she were precious to him. He was too close for her to see him well.

But she had studied his picture and knew he was a striking man. His amazing green eyes were deep-set. His gaze intense. His chin was strong. His lips finely shaped. But he hadn't bothered to smile for the camera. She imagined that a smile would completely transform him.

Now she could tell that his frame was tall and strong as he wrapped her close, and she couldn't get the notion out of her head that he had held her many times before, his body as familiar as her own.

Nonsense. She had never met him in person until a few moments ago. But she had come to know him through their correspondence.

She let her head sag to his broad shoulder, clinging to him for long moments before he cleared his throat. "Let's go."

"Yes," she managed as she came back to her senses. They were still in danger, and she was going all dreamy on him.

As promised, he turned away from her.

"Circle my waist," he said gruffly.

She did as he asked, wrapping her arms around him. When she realized her grip was too low and her hands were pressed over the fly of his slacks, she jerked, then quickly moved her arms a couple of inches higher.

A fresh surge of water tore at her, trying to break her grip on his waist. It almost did, and she was glad the rope bound them together.

She gritted her teeth as they inched toward blacktop. He was using the rope, pulling them along hand over hand. She hoped he'd tied the other end to something solid.

He didn't spare the breath to talk now. It was all he could do to keep them moving toward shore.

Something large slammed past them, and she gasped from the impact.

"Are you all right?" he asked urgently.

"Yes."

Redoubling his efforts, he hauled them the last few yards through the water and out of the deluge.

Breathless, they both sprawled on dry land, panting.

For long moments all she could do was lie still with her eyes closed, grateful to be on a solid surface again.

When she realized that the solid surface was Andre Gascon's body, she tensed, then tried to push herself away. She managed to put a few inches of space between them before the rope pulled her back, and she flopped onto his chest again.

"Go ahead, use me for a trampoline," he said.

She was icy cold from the water, but she had to laugh.

The comment was so typical of the dry humor that she'd enjoyed in his e-mails. He'd struck her as a man who used humor to defuse a tense situation. Apparently he was still doing it.

Large hands moved over her back and shoulders, untangling her from the rope, then lifted her up and onto her feet. She blinked into the intense green eyes she remembered from the picture.

His dark hair was plastered to his head, his T-shirt to his chest. When she wavered on her feet, he scooped her up and strode away from the water. She anchored her hands on his muscular shoulders as he carried her to an SUV parked on the shoulder, well out of the reach of the flood that surged across the road.

Even though he'd been in the water, a pungent aroma clung to him, as if he wore some kind of strong aftershave that she couldn't identify. It was a natural fragrance that drew her the way the man had drawn her.

Setting her in the passenger seat, he worked the lever to push the seat back so she could stretch out her legs.

She threw her head back and closed her eyes, contemplating her narrow escape.

"Are you all right?" he asked, his voice gritty.

"I...think...so," she answered between panting breaths. Opening her eyes, she stared into his face, taking in the stark lines. "But I wouldn't have been, if you hadn't come along. Thank you," she murmured.

"I'm glad I got here in time," he answered, the words carrying a depth of feeling that overwhelmed her.

Perhaps she was struggling to put some distance be-tween them when she said, "This isn't a very auspicious way for you to meet your private detective."

"Don't worry about that." He looked across the water toward her rental car. "How did you end up in a ditch?"

She huffed out a breath. "My brakes failed. I couldn't keep the car on the road. Of course, that was after two men from town started following me and I sped up to get away."

He swore under his breath. "What men?"

"Two guys from the gas station where I stopped to fill my tank. When I told them I was coming here, I caused a little bit of a stir."

"You should have kept that information to yourself," he muttered.

"I was gauging their reaction," she countered.

"Well, you have it. They ran you off the road. They're getting bolder," he said, his tone turning rough with anger.

"We'll deal with that later. How did you know to come looking for me?"

"You were later than I expected," he answered. "I thought I'd better see if you were in trouble."

"From what?" she asked, struggling to keep her teeth from chattering.

"The rain. We've had some flash floods like this. I wasn't thinking anyone would follow you from town."

"They didn't stay around."

"Why not?"

"A jaguar scared them off," she said, suddenly want-ing his reaction to that statement.

His expression turned fierce. "As I told you in my correspondence, someone in town is playing jaguar."

"That may be true. But I saw a...a real one," she answered, losing the battle to keep her teeth from clanking together.

"That may be, but the animal isn't the problem," he said, then gave her an appraising look as he changed the subject. "You need to get warm. You'd better get out of your wet clothes. What's left of them."

She'd been so grateful to be back on dry land that any thought of her appearance had fled her mind. Now she looked down at herself, seeing her bare legs, then her blouse clinging wetly to her breasts, plainly showing the darker outline of her tightened nipples.

Embarrassed, she stammered, "I...I need—"

"Clothing," he supplied. "In the back I have some things I was taking to the church sale." Climbing out again, he went around to the back of the vehicle. She watched him rummaging through large plastic bags, heard him muttering.

When he returned, he was holding out a lady's robe, made of soft ecru silk, the front panels decorated with delicate embroidery.

She reached out, stroking the fabric, trying to keep her fingers from trembling, aware of his eyes on her.

"This is beautiful. You were getting rid of it?" she asked, her voice turning soft.

"Janet said it was in an old trunk," he answered, sounding offhand. Yet she sensed a current of meaning running below the surface of his words. When he laid the robe across her knees, it felt warm and alive against her chilled flesh. And dangerous.

Janet. His housekeeper. He'd mentioned her in his correspondence.

She continued to stroke the fabric. The robe would

cover her; still, she heard herself asking, "Do you have something else?"

He tipped his head to one side, watching her. "You could try one of my shirts and a pair of my pants if you like the ragamuffin look."

"I'll pass on that," she answered, trying to match his light tone.

"Since it's stopped raining, I can give you some privacy."

Before she could answer, he strode around the SUV, and she saw him rummaging again in the bags. This time he pulled out a T-shirt and jeans much like the wet ones he was wearing.

Standing out on the road, behind the vehicle, he pulled his sodden shirt over his head, and she found herself staring at the mat of dark hair spreading across his chest, before dragging her eyes away. He said he wanted to give her privacy. She should do the same.

She looked down at the robe still warming her lap. The garment was old and beautiful, like something from a vintage clothing store. Very appealing. Yet as she stared at it, she was oddly reluctant to put it on.

A thought lodged itself in her head. *If you put on the robe, nothing will ever be the same again.*

Nonsense. It was just an old item of clothing. As good as anything else to cover her goose-bumped flesh. Probably it had belonged to his grandmother or some long-forgotten female guest.

Quickly, while he was changing his own clothing, she struggled with the buttons of her blouse. Leaving on her damp panties and bra, she put her arms through the sleeves of the robe, then closed the front and began working the buttons.

All at once her fingers became numb, and her head muzzy.

Delayed reaction from almost being swept downstream, she reasoned. Because the world was spinning around her, she leaned back against the seat and closed her eyes.

For a moment she felt as if she was floating away from the earth, tethered by only the barest of threads. Dreamily she slid her hand down the front of the garment, sending little currents of heat over her skin.

Exhaustion had her drifting, somewhere between sleep and wakefulness. Then a deep, masculine voice called her name, bringing her back to the world. Only it wasn't her name—or the twenty-first century. Was it?

"Linette."

Her eyes blinked open. The sun had dipped low behind the trees at the edge of the clearing. She was sitting on the porch, in the old rocking chair that Papa had made. A bowl sat in her lap. A big wooden bowl of beans she was supposed to be snapping. But really, she had come out here as she had on many evenings, hoping that her love would ride this way again.

She looked toward the shadows, prepared for disappointment. But this time she saw him, and her heart leaped inside her chest. "Andre."

He didn't venture any closer to the cabin in the bayou, and she knew the reason. He shouldn't be here. He shouldn't be seeking her out. She had told him it was wrong. Told herself. Yet here he was. Come from the plantation house to her little cabin in the bayou.

He could probably guess that her papa was out checking his traps. But did he know that her momma had gone to take care of a sick friend?

Despite all the words of denial that had passed her lips, she set down the bowl on the gray boards of the porch and hurried down the steps, her long skirts swishing around her legs as she picked up speed.

Avoiding the vegetable garden, she dashed into the trees. Into his arms. He caught her against his broad chest, hugging her to him.

"I thought we agreed that you wouldn't come back," she said in a breathy whisper.

"I shouldn't have. But I couldn't stay away."

"Thank the saints for that," she said.

"I am not good for you."

Probably he was right. But now that he held her in his arms, everything felt more right than it had in weeks.

She hung on to him, feeling her heart racing, closing her eyes as his strong hands stroked up and down her arms.

"I had to hold you. Just hold you."

"Only that?" she teased, then tipped her face up, silently asking for his kiss.

He was glad to oblige, lowering his mouth, brushing his lips back and forth. She closed her eyes and wrapped her arms around his neck, clinging to him as he moved his mouth more firmly against hers. They had done this before, but she knew he had always set limits on himself.

Now she wanted to push him past that limit. When she boldly pressed her body against his, he answered with a low groan that made her knees weak. Gathering her more tightly in his arms, he slid his tongue along the seam of her lips. She opened instantly to him, and his head angled for deeper possession. When his tongue circled hers in a seductive dance, she felt her head spin.

His hands moved restlessly up and down her back. Through her skirt and petticoats, she felt a hard rod pressing against her. She knew what that was. Knew what it meant, because her mother had warned her that when a man's body changed like that, he would be dangerous. He might try to bed her. If he did that, no other man would want her for a wife.

She knew her mother was right. She knew it when she was away from Andre, when she was thinking clearly. He wanted to make love with her, and that was wrong. But when she was with him, her own desire leaped up to meet his.

He lifted his mouth, and she moaned in protest. She wanted more. So much more.

They were both breathing hard now.

In the good-girl part of her mind, she knew she shouldn't be doing this. She had warned herself often enough that the daughter of Jacques Sonnier had no place with the son of Henri Gascon. He was from the plantation. She was from the backcountry. His family had wealth and power. Hers scraped out an existence for themselves as best they could.

Andre Gascon must marry a woman from another powerful family. And Linette Sonnier must wed a man of her own station.

All of that was the truth. But none of it made any difference now that she was in his arms.

When he bent to kiss her again and stroked the sensitive inside of her lip, a shiver traveled over her body.

His hand slid up her ribs, sending heat through her, then eased inward, brushing the side of her breast, creating a jolt of hot sensation.

Their eyes met, and she saw desire. He wanted her.

And what he was doing was making her forget she must tell him to stop.

She dragged in a breath. But before she could speak, a voice was interrupting them.

Her father? Had he come back and caught them?

Fear crackled through her.

But it wasn't her father. It was someone else. Far away. Too far to reach her and Andre.

"Morgan? Morgan, are you all right?" The words floated toward her from across the bayou. Floated on time and space.

She longed to stay where she was. In his arms, wrapped in the pleasant but pungent aroma that clung to his skin. His scent. For the rest of her life, she would know him by that familiar scent.

Then his hand closed over her shoulder, his fingers burning into her flesh as he gently shook her.

Her eyes snapped open, and she found herself staring up at a face that was the same as her lover's, yet not the same.

Chapter Three

Morgan gripped the edge of the car seat, trying to anchor herself, trying to remember who she was and where she was.

Her name floated into her mind.

She was Linette Sonnier.

Linette.

For a moment it felt right. Good. Comforting. She liked being the woman in the dream. Then her sense of rightness was shattered as her consciousness swept her back into the terror of the floodwaters.

In her mind, the current caught her and carried her away. She opened her mouth to scream, but no sound came out.

God, no. She was going to die.

She fought the force of the flood. Fought the terror.

"Morgan! Morgan!"

Her eyes flew open. She wasn't in the water. She was safe in the car. She was Morgan Kirkland, wearing a borrowed robe. She wasn't someone named Linette.

Relief flooded through her as she clutched the importance of that fact to her breast.

She was Morgan Kirkland. She hadn't drowned. She was safe. And as she absorbed that blessed fact, others followed. She worked for the Light Street Detective Agency. She had come to the Louisiana bayou country on assignment for a man called Andre Gascon.

And he was standing beside her. He was the one who had pulled her out of the water.

She looked up at him and blinked.

"Are you all right?" he asked, and again she was thrown into confusion as images blended and reformed.

He was Andre. Not the man in her vision, but the man who had hired her for an undercover assignment. But she must remember there was another man named Andre. Long ago. And she loved him.

No! She loved her husband—Trevor Kirkland. She tried to hold on to his image. But it was like trying to hold on to a picture printed in water.

Deliberately, as she had so many times over the past two years, she brought back the last glorious weekend they had spent together down at the shore.

They had taken a few quiet walks on the beach. But mostly they had spent hours in an expensive motel room, making love, ordering Chinese food and pizza and champagne.

He had said he would come back to her. And she had believed him. Then she'd heard about an uprising at a prison compound in Afghanistan, and she'd prayed that Trevor wasn't there, that he was all right. But when two men in business suits had come to her house, her whole body had gone cold. She'd known what they were going to tell her—that her husband was dead. Nothing had mattered after that. Not her friends. Not her job. Not her own life.

Now, suddenly, everything had changed, and she didn't like it.

"Morgan, are you all right?"

A man was speaking. His name was Andre. The owner of Belle Vista.

Pushing herself up straighter, she cleared her throat and gave the only answer she could, the only answer she wanted to give. "I'm fine."

"You looked…spacey."

"I'm fine!" she repeated, this time snapping out the words. She had always known exactly who she was and what she believed.

And she would not allow herself to be confused.

Yet she recognized that something had happened inside her mind. Something beyond her control.

It had to do with the robe she was wearing. She had put it on, and her consciousness had slipped away from the here and now.

She couldn't explain it, but cold fingers of fear clawed at her insides. Grimly she shoved them away, as she had shoved so many emotions away.

A man stood over her, his face anxious. She had dreamed of him a little while ago. Well, not him. Someone who looked a lot like him. A guy with the same name, but dressed in old-fashioned shirt, pants and boots, like a country gentleman from the late-nineteenth century.

She gave a small mental shrug. Why try to fix the episode in time? It was just a dream she'd made up because she was having a bad time here and now in the Louisiana backcountry.

And exhaustion had a lot to do with it, she silently added. She was so wrung out, she'd fallen asleep for a few minutes and she'd tried to escape.

Deep down she didn't quite believe that explanation.

What would Andre Gascon say if she told the story to him?

Unable to meet his gaze, she turned her head toward the water. It still flowed across the road, but not as deeply or as swiftly. Soon the floodwaters would subside, leaving no indication that she'd almost been swept into oblivion.

She shivered, knowing she was wildly off balance, and not just from the near-death experience.

Andre walked around the car and slipped behind the wheel, then shut the door. In the close confines of the car, she breathed in the pungent aroma that clung to him. It was very appealing.

"What kind of aftershave do you use?" she asked.

"Aftershave?"

"Sorry. I was just thinking I liked the way you smelled," she said, aware that she had shoved her foot farther into her mouth.

Ignoring the comment, he said, "We should go home. It's going to be dark soon."

"I'll feel pretty silly arriving in this robe," she muttered.

"It's better than arriving in just a wet blouse."

He was right. "We could wait until the water goes down. Then we could get my suitcase."

"That will take too long. The bayou can be dangerous after dark. Especially now."

"Why now?"

"Snakes could have washed up on the road."

Starting the engine, he backed up, then turned the wheel. On the narrow pavement, he needed several maneuvers to reverse his direction. But finally he was able to make a U-turn and head toward Belle Vista.

The sun was sinking toward the horizon when they turned in at a small sign that announced the plantation. The one-lane drive wound through the bayou, the gloom closing in on them as they made their way deeper into the natural area.

He was driving fast now, turning the scenery to a dark blur.

"Slow down," she said, hearing the thin quality of her own voice.

"I know this road," he answered. "I've lived here all my life."

Since he was obviously eager to get home, she switched tactics. "How much land do you have?" she asked.

He sighed, making her think he would have preferred silence. But he answered the question. "Around two hundred acres."

She made a whistling noise. "That's amazing."

"Instead of selling it off, we kept it in the family." He laughed. "Of course a lot of it is an underwater paradise half the year."

She sat tensely in her seat as they roared around another curve and emerged from the wilderness onto a double-wide drive. Willow trees on either side led to a large house. As they drew closer, her breath caught.

He'd told her about his estate and sent her pictures. But nothing had adequately prepared her for the reality of Belle Vista. She stared at the graceful stucco building with its twin curved staircases and two-story porticos surrounded by manicured gardens. In the glow from the setting sun, it looked like a jewel that had been lovingly polished.

"Your home is stunning," she breathed.

"Thank you," he answered, sounding genuinely pleased. "It was getting a little run-down. I wanted to restore it to its former glory."

As they pulled to a stop in the circular drive, she glanced around at what looked like an oasis in the middle of the bayou.

"Your gardener must put in long days keeping all this up," she said.

"I do it myself," he answered.

"All of it?"

"Yes."

"Isn't that a lot of work?"

"I'll tell you about it tomorrow," he answered, tense again.

"Okay," she said carefully, wondering what was bothering him now. Maybe the same thing that was bothering her. She'd gotten physically close to him a while ago. Maybe he was having a similar reaction.

She gave him a sideways glance as he stepped out of the car and turned toward the sunset. "We made it. But you need to get into the house."

Quickly he exited the SUV, then came around to yank open her door. "Come inside."

After her narrow escape from death, she wanted to linger in the driveway, watch the sun set over the trees and simply enjoy the wonder of being alive. But the tension radiating from the man standing next to her seeped into the bucolic picture.

Aware once again that she was barefoot and wearing a borrowed robe, she followed him up one of the curving staircases to a wide porch where he ushered her through double front doors.

They stopped in a large center hall, lit by a lamp on a marble-topped chest. She was craning her neck, looking up at the floating staircase when the sound of footsteps made her jerk around. She saw Andre striding rapidly toward the back of the house, disappearing into the darkness at the rear of the hall.

"Wait! Where are you going?"

He left her standing where she was. Alone and a bit confused.

She waited for him to come back. But as the seconds ticked by, she figured that wasn't going to happen.

What was wrong with him? Had he undergone a personality transplant since their e-mails? Or had he carefully hidden the real Andre Gascon from her? Perhaps he dealt with people better from long distances. Was that it?

Because she couldn't simply stand where she was, she finally started toward the back of the house. Daylight was fading quickly and there were no windows in the hall. The farther she got from the side lights framing the front door, the more difficult it became to see where she was going.

Then a door in front of her suddenly opened, and the blast of light made her gasp.

Someone else made a startled sound, then stopped short.

"Is that you, Ms. Kirkland?"

"Yes."

A light snapped on, and she found herself facing a short, gray-haired woman wearing a flowered housedress over her thin body. She looked to be in her early sixties. "Are you Janet Laveren, Mr. Gascon's house-keeper?" she asked.

"Yes." The woman spoke slowly, clearly looking Morgan up and down in surprise. "Well, bless your heart. You look a sight. Why are you wearing that robe?"

"I know I look a bit…odd," Morgan answered, running her hand through her hair. It was stiff from the water, and she hated to think about the picture she made. "I…I was caught in a flash flood. Mr. Gascon rescued me."

"Thank the Lord!"

"Yes." Her hand fluttered. "Most of my clothes were swept away by the current. So Mr. Gascon dug this out of a bag of donations he was taking to a church sale."

Feeling as if she was babbling, yet unable to stop herself, Morgan went on quickly, "I wanted to get my suit-case out of the car, but the water blocked the road, and my car was on the other side. Then Mr. Gascon said we had to get back here before dark."

"He would," Janet agreed.

"Where did he go?"

The housekeeper hesitated for a moment. "He's never available at night," she finally said.

"Why?"

"This is his private time."

"Oh," was all Morgan could dredge up. She wanted to tell Janet Laveren that Mr. Gascon was turning out to be a pretty strange man. But that hardly seemed like the way to start a relationship with the only other person who lived in the plantation house.

The woman's voice softened. "It sounds like you had a close call."

"Yes."

The housekeeper was inspecting her closely. "Your hair is shorter than hers," she murmured, "But your eyes are the right color."

"Who?"

"Sorry," she said quickly, "I'm old, and my mind starts to wander. I'm glad you're all right. I was told to expect you today. Then, when it got late and you didn't show up, I didn't know if you were still coming."

"Well, I'm here now," Morgan answered automatically, touching her hair, wanting to go back to the previous few moments of conversation. But she suspected she wasn't going to get Janet to tell her what she was talking about. The woman might be old, but her gaze was piercing.

Raising her chin, Morgan went on with her own explanation. "I was hired to catalog the books in the library for Mr. Gascon," she added, giving the cover story she'd used in town.

The woman's gaze remained steady. "You don't have to give me that story, child. I know why you're really here. Andre and I discussed it."

"Oh," Morgan managed. Gascon hadn't told her anyone else knew about their real arrangement. But apparently he'd taken Janet into his confidence.

"I have some seafood stew waiting on the back of the stove. You told Andre you like it."

"Yes," she murmured.

In fact, she and Andre had talked about food in their correspondence. She knew he loved the spicy Cajun dishes his housekeeper made. And she'd been looking forward to trying them.

She let the woman lead her down the hall. As soon

as they stepped through a swinging door into the kitchen, a delicious aroma filled the air.

"It smells wonderful," she murmured.

"I know you must be worn-out. Please sit down." The woman gestured toward a square wooden table that looked like a restored antique.

Morgan dropped into one of the pressed-back chairs and looked around. The table might be antique, but everything else was brand-new. The large room was lined with cherry wood cabinets, the countertops were a beautifully polished granite and the restaurant-grade range was stainless steel, matching the refrigerator and the dishwasher.

Janet ladled thick red stew over fluffy white rice, then brought the bowl to the table.

"Thank you," Morgan said, spooning some up and blowing to cool it down before tasting it.

Janet was standing watching her, pleating the edge of her apron with her hand. "How is it?"

"Delicious." Morgan smiled, trying to put them both at ease and thinking that praising the woman's cooking was a good way to ingratiate herself. She was hoping Janet would be a good source of information. Or was she too loyal to Andre Gascon to be entirely honest?

"What can I get you to drink?"

"Tea. If that's not too much trouble."

"Oh, no. Regular black tea or herbal?"

"Regular is fine."

The woman bustled to the sink, drew water and set a kettle on the stove. Then she got out a box of tea bags—English imports, Morgan noted.

"How long have you worked for Mr. Gascon?" Morgan asked.

"Since he was a little boy."

Morgan nodded. After eating another spoonful of stew, she asked, "So I guess you're worried about what's been going on in the swamp and the way the town is blaming the incidents on Mr. Gascon."

"The town is making a mistake," she snapped. "But the problem in the bayou will sort itself out." To punctuate the statement, the kettle began to whistle, and Janet snatched it off the burner, then poured hot water over a tea bag.

"How do you take your tea?" she asked.

"Just sugar," Morgan answered, hoping sweetened tea might soothe her.

She had taken a couple of sips when a bloodcurdling roar from outside made her go rigid. Her hand shook, and tea slopped into her saucer. Her gaze shot to Janet. Both of them had gone absolutely still, staring at each other across eight feet of suddenly charged space.

Morgan spoke first. "What was that?" she managed, thinking that her nerves of steel were being tested again.

"An animal in the swamp," Janet answered, her voice only the slightest bit shaky.

The answer wasn't good enough, not when goose bumps peppered Morgan's arms. "What animal?" she pressed.

"I don't know. I mean, Mr. Gascon and his father before him warned me to stay inside at night."

Morgan sat at the table, her breath shallow, as she waited to hear the roar again. When the silence lengthened, she gave Janet a direct look. "I didn't tell you everything that happened on my way from the airport. Before I arrived here, I stopped in St. Germaine to get gas. After I left town, some men from the gas station ran me off the road. That was how I happened to get caught in that flash flood."

"Oh, my word!"

"Before the flood, an animal came out of the swamp and chased the men away. Well, not chased them, to be perfectly accurate. They saw him and ran."

"What animal?"

"A jaguar."

A look of pure shock sharpened Janet's features, a look Morgan knew the housekeeper couldn't be faking. "Are you sure?" the woman breathed.

"As sure as I can be."

"That's very unusual," Janet murmured, obviously more in control now.

Morgan nodded. "What does it mean?" she asked.

The woman waited several seconds before answering. Her voice turned low and serious. "That you're under the protection of Belle Vista."

"How?" Morgan demanded. "I mean, I understood from Mr. Gascon that the cat was just a myth."

"Myth or not, that cat guards us," Janet said. Then, changing the subject abruptly, she said, "You've had a hard day. You're probably tired. Let me show you to your room."

Morgan was dying to bombard the woman with questions until she got a better answer. But she was sure she'd have to win her trust before she got the real scoop.

And to be honest, it *had* been a long day, and Morgan wasn't betting on her effectiveness at subtle interrogation.

"Okay."

As soon as she agreed, the housekeeper visibly relaxed. "I chose a lovely room for you. Let me show you upstairs."

Morgan followed Janet up the curved staircase and down the hall to the third door on the right. The room beyond *was* lovely. With its canopy bed, marble-topped dresser and tall armoire, it looked like something out of a set for a Civil War movie.

No, wait. They called it something else down here. The War of Northern Aggression.

"You have a private bathroom," Janet said, opening another door. Like the kitchen, it was very modern with a huge soaking tub, a separate shower and a large pedestal sink.

A wave of fatigue hit Morgan with a body blow, and she swayed on her feet.

Janet gave her a sympathetic look. "You must be exhausted, child. Get a good night's rest, and we'll see you in the morning."

Suddenly Morgan remembered what she was wearing. Gesturing toward the cast-off robe, she said, "I— I don't have anything else to put on."

"I'm sure Andre can get your suitcase from the car in the morning. I hope you don't mind sticking with what you have for now."

Morgan did mind, but she said, "No, that's fine."

After the housekeeper left her alone, she washed her swamp-soaked underwear in the sink, then hung it over a towel bar before taking the fastest shower on record. She was swaying on her feet by the time she got out, toweled dry and used the hair dryer she found on one of the shelves.

She'd left the robe hanging on the back of the door, and the idea of putting it back on brought a strange, tingling sensation to her skin. But it was either that or go to bed naked, and she certainly wasn't going to do that in a strange house where her host had disappeared and wild animals prowled the grounds outside. What did people do if there was a fire, she wondered. Run outside and take their chances in the zoo?

The image made her giggle. It wasn't a pleasant sound. She'd lived through a hell of a day, and she knew she was close to the edge of hysteria. She needed to sleep, then maybe she would feel better in the morning.

Snatching up the robe, she pulled it on and did up the buttons with clumsy fingers. She was in bad shape. Worse than any time she could remember in recent memory. She had never thought that she was afraid of the dark, but in this unfamiliar place, she wanted to be able to see where she was if she woke in the night, so she left the bathroom light on and left the door ajar.

Satisfied that the light wasn't bright enough to keep her awake, she hurried across the room to the bed.

While she'd been in the bathroom, Janet had turned back the lacy spread, revealing a light blanket and crisp white sheets.

Gratefully Morgan climbed between them, made the pillows comfortable under her neck and closed her eyes.

On edge, she lay in the darkness, staring at the canopy above her head, feeling as if she'd stepped out of her old life and into another world where she had no idea what to expect from one moment to the next. It was important to think about Trevor. After he'd been killed, her grief had been like barbwire twisting in her guts. The pain had dulled over time, but she still missed him. She still knew that she'd never feel the same about any other man.

In the darkness she called up scenes from their life together. She'd brought Trevor to meet Mom and Dad. She'd always known that her churchgoing parents were protective of her. But Trevor knew how to win them over. He and Dad had gone fishing together. They'd puttered around in the garage, working on Dad's prize 1958 Thunderbird. Trevor knew how to charm her father—and her mother, too. Every time Mom set a dish in front of him, he'd extravagantly praised her cooking. And he'd bought her candy and flowers as though she were the one he was courting.

She smiled, remembering how well he got along with people. How smart he'd been. How much fun. How he hadn't had any of that male chauvinism that infected so many men in the intelligence services.

They'd talked about getting out of the spook business and opening their own security company. They'd talked about children, but she'd known deep down that wasn't really what Trevor wanted. He was too much of an adventurer, while she'd secretly longed to put down roots. After he'd died, she'd thought that if she'd had his child, she wouldn't have lost everything.

Remembering Trevor helped ground her. She was in a strange place, but she could always rely on the skills he'd helped her hone.

Outside, the sounds of the night lulled her. Nothing louder than the buzz of insects, or frogs calling to their mates.

This was Andre Gascon's territory. He'd described it in loving detail over the past few weeks, made it come alive in her imagination. He'd said that in the quiet of the night, the sounds of the bayou were like a natural symphony. And as she lay in bed, she had to agree.

He'd made her long to settle down in a place like this, if she were secretly honest.

Feeling more peaceful than she had all day, she finally fell asleep. For a while she was deep in oblivion. Then she woke up. Well, not exactly woke, because she knew she was dreaming. And once again, she knew she was someone else. A woman named Linette who lived in a small cabin at the edge of the bayou. It was like the dream she'd had when she'd fallen asleep in the car.

"No," she whispered. "Let me go. I don't want to be here."

"Yes, you do," a voice whispered in her head. "Yes, you do. This is right for you. You're home now."

Whether she wanted it or not, it seemed that she had no choice. Once again she was sitting on the front porch, waiting for a man named Andre. Not the man who had requested the services of the Light Street Agency. Another man who had lived long ago. She was back there with him, in his world.

He was wearing an old-fashioned riding outfit, and he had come on horseback, along the trail from Belle Vista.

Belle Vista? The same house where Morgan Kirkland slept?

Yes.

The knowledge was confusing, unsettling. But she accepted it, just as she finally accepted who she was—Linette Sonnier.

Not just accepted. She was glad to be here. Happy.

She watched him stop for a moment at the edge of the clearing, barely visible from the porch. Then he beckoned to her before turning his horse into the shadows of the trees.

Papa was out in the bayou again. But Momma was

home. Linette cast a quick glance over her shoulder, then quickly climbed down off the porch and gathered up the skirt of her long dress as she ran into the shadows, following Andre and the horse.

Finally he stopped and dismounted in a spot where the sunshine filtered through the leaves. After tying his huge black stallion to a tupelo tree, he turned to her. The horse nickered in greeting. Like his master, he knew her well. With a smile she turned to stroke her hand along his nose, wishing she had some carrots with her. "Hello, Richelieu."

"Don't you have a greeting for *me?*" the man asked, amusement in his voice.

"Oh, yes."

He moved beside her, opening his hand, and she saw a carrot. When he offered it to her, she took it, then flattened her hand, feeding the treat to the horse.

"He likes you. So do I. Well, a bit more than like. I love you."

The words made her heart squeeze, yet she whispered, "You shouldn't."

"I can't help myself."

The words were harder for her to say. Instead she turned, holding out her arms, and he came into them, hugging her tightly and kissing her cheek before setting her a little away.

"I didn't just bring a present for you to feed the horse. I brought you something from New Orleans." Reaching in his pocket again, he held up a small box. When she only stared at it, he removed the top and took out a gold locket hanging on a slender gold chain.

She reached to touch the beautiful piece, stroking the engraved work on the front of the locket. She had never held anything so precious or so finely made in her life.

She shook her head in regret. "I can't take anything like that from you."

"Of course you can."

Lifting out the locket, he held it in his hand, then sprang the catch. Inside were two miniature portraits. They had been done by a skilled artist, because she recognized the people immediately and gasped.

"You and me."

"Oui."

"But how?"

"Do you remember that man who came to your father's house, saying he was traveling through the area?"

"Yes."

"You gave him a meal and he kept staring at you. You told me he made you uncomfortable."

She laughed. *"Oui.* I wondered what he wanted."

"I am sorry I distressed you, *chère.* But he was the artist who painted these portraits. I needed him to see you, so he would understand your beauty for himself. So I sent him into the bayou. You should have heard him complain about having to travel to the backcountry."

"Oh, Andre." She stopped, overwhelmed with emotion, needing to clear her throat before she continued. "You went to a lot of trouble for me."

"I wanted to give you a present that would mean something—to both of us."

She closed the cover with regret, then stroked her thumb over the shiny surface. "My father would never let me wear this. I'd have to hide it from him."

"I know that. Until I get his permission to court you, you can wear it under your dress, next to your silky skin." As he spoke, he took the locket from her suddenly stiff fingers, reached around her neck and fastened the clasp. He looked for a moment at the locket resting against her bodice. Then he gravely opened the first two buttons and slipped the locket inside. It was hot against her skin, hot like his touch, as he opened two more buttons, just that simple act sending currents of heat through her body.

"Andre," she sighed as he leaned down, then stroked his lips gently against the tender skin below her neck. "Oh, Andre."

"I will have you for my wife," he whispered.

She wanted that to be true. So much. At night, in her narrow bed, she longed to reach out and find herself in a wider bed—with him beside her. But she didn't think it could ever happen. He was like the lord of the manor and she was one of the peasants. If she was going to have anything with him, she must grab what she could, while she could. Well, not everything. Only what wouldn't get her in real trouble.

When he opened his saddlebag, she looked at him questioningly. He only smiled at her and led her farther into the bayou.

They came to a place under a spreading oak tree, where she saw he had gathered leaves and moss into a soft pile. And when he opened the saddlebag, she saw that he had brought a coverlet with him.

Her pulse was pounding as she watched him spread it on the leaves, making a bed. When he turned back to her, his face was serious. "I want us to be comfortable when I take you in my arms."

"I…" She had been bold in kissing him, letting him touch her in forbidden places. But lying down with him was something she knew went too far.

"You are thinking we shouldn't do that," he said.

She could only nod.

"I know why it's a bad idea for you. But, *chère,* I would never hurt you. Never do anything we shouldn't."

They had already done things they shouldn't, if she were strictly honest with herself. Yet when he sat down and held out his hand, she took it and sat beside him, feeling her back stiffen as she tried to keep from shaking.

And she knew he could feel it, too.

"You're right to be nervous. But you never have to be frightened of me. I respect you too much to hurt you."

"Respect? How can you respect a woman who is sitting with you on a bed under an oak tree."

"Because I love you," he said again. *"Je t'aime,"* he repeated.

"Oh, Andre!"

"I'm not saying that because I am going to force you into anything," he added hastily.

"I know." She dragged in a breath and let it out in a rush, then said the words that had been bottled up inside her since the first afternoon they had met out by the old fallen tree. "I love you so much."

"My love. My angel. I ached to hear that. Thank you for being brave enough to tell me."

"I shouldn't."

"Oui. You should. I live for the time we can be together as man and wife."

It was the same for her. She dared to let joy leap inside her.

He squeezed her hand, kissed her cheek, his lips soft and gentle. When he turned her to him, she let him gather her into his arms, let him run his tongue along her closed lips. She should keep them closed. But she couldn't. She opened for him, glorying in the sensation of his tongue caressing the inside of her lips, her teeth, then engaging her own tongue in a slow, erotic tryst that made her blood heat and her pulse pound.

While he kissed her, he stroked his hands along her ribs as he had done before, then slowly slid them inward, teasing the sides of her breasts, then finally cupping them in his hands through the fabric of her bodice and chemise.

She should stop him. He shouldn't touch her like that. But she was helpless to say the word no.

Instead she turned more fully toward him, a small sound rising in her throat as he caressed her there. Then he did something new, his fingers brushing over her hardened nipples, making heat leap inside her. Helplessly, she felt a pleading sound rise in her throat.

"Andre. Oh, Andre."

"You like that?"

"Oh, yes. I didn't know anything could feel that good."

"There's more, love." He gathered her close, then lay back on the coverlet, taking her with him, holding her in his arms, pulling her body against his, her skirts tangling around their legs as he rocked with her.

Flames lapped at her. The flames of hell, she thought. But she didn't care. There was only this moment, this man and the desperation they shared.

He rolled to his back, pulling her on top of him, stroking his hands down her body so that every aching inch of her was pressed to his.

They were both shaking with strong emotions. All she could think was that the clothing they wore was in the way. And she knew at that moment she would have let him do anything he wanted with her.

"Andre, I need…" She wasn't even sure how to finish the sentence.

"I know, love. I know." He adjusted her body, so that her aching center was pressed to the hard rod of flesh at the front of his britches. It felt so good there. No, wonderful.

"Oh!" Unable to stop herself, she moved against him, her desperation rising as his hands pressed her to him, then played with her breasts through the fabric covering them.

She heard herself moan. She knew she had turned into a total wanton as her movements became frantic, as she strove for something she couldn't name. And then a burst of pleasure grabbed her, making her call out with the wonder of it.

She was left limp and panting, her head pressed to his shoulder as he stroked her back and tangled his fingers in her hair.

"What did you do to me?"

"I gave you—"

Before he could finish his answer, a sound intruded into the dream. A woman's voice, chanting, pulling Morgan away from Andre as surely as if strong fingers were tangled in her hair, yanking painfully. Yanking her back to reality.

Chapter Four

Morgan woke, breathing hard and feeling disoriented. Her body was flush with the aftermath of sexual release—a sensation she hadn't experienced in a long time.

In the dark she felt her face heat as wisps of the erotic dream drifted through her mind.

Where was she? In a bed. She had been sleeping. Now she was awake.

Something had snapped her out of the dream. A sound.

It filtered into her consciousness, making the hairs on the backs of her arms stand up and her skin tingle. It was a woman's voice, chanting to the sound of a drum.

Out in the humid night.

Morgan strained her ears, trying to figure out the words. But she couldn't make any sense of them, and finally she came to the conclusion that they were in some language she didn't understand. An ancient language that sounded rough and primitive and evil.

She shivered. Evil. Yes, the chant sounded like pure evil. Meant to do harm.

To her? Or to Andre Gascon?

Suddenly Morgan was very glad that she was safe inside the house, not out in the midnight garden.

Slipping from the bed, she glided to the window, staying to the side as she peeked out. Moonlight silvered the garden. From the safety of her bedroom, she searched the grounds of Belle Vista.

She was in rural Louisiana, she reminded herself. At the Gascon family home. She had come here because Andre Gascon had asked for a private detective to figure out who was killing people in the swamp near his home. Killing people and making it look as if a big cat had done it. And somehow that was supposed to be his fault. She hadn't quite figured out how that fit into the scenario.

But maybe he was doing something illegal with animals. Maybe he had a zoo out there in the bayou, and he was letting the residents roam around at night. She'd come up with that theory last week, and it made as much sense as anything else.

He had hired her to get to the bottom of his problem. Or so he said. Perhaps he had brought her here to use her in some way.

The thought was ludicrous. Use her for what?

Still, she sensed he might not have been entirely honest about his motives. And his having hired her didn't restrict her to any limits he set. She would look for that zoo. But not now. Not out in the darkness, when her head was pounding in the same insistent rhythm as the drum she heard outside.

She pressed the palm of her hand against her throbbing temple. It only gave a focus to the pain.

As her eyes probed the shadows beyond the lawn,

she froze. All at once what had looked like tree branches resolved itself into another shape. There was someone out there—the long, lithe figure of a woman. Chanting and banging on a small drum.

Morgan had been standing at the side of the window. Now she felt a strange compulsion to show herself. Stepping in front of the glass, she faced the darkness.

As if the strange visitor knew she was being watched, she looked up toward the window where Morgan stood. They were too far away and it was too dark for their gazes to meet. But as she stared at the figure, her mind flashed back to the house on the edge of town—the one with the sign in the window that said Voodoo Priestess. The one where she'd seen someone watching her.

Were they one and the same? It was impossible to tell in the dark. But Morgan was trained to take in the details of a person's appearance. This individual seemed to be about the same height, weight and shape.

The voodoo priestess, if that was who she was, tipped her head to one side. In acknowledgment? Or triumph?

Morgan didn't know. But she felt a profound sense of relief when the woman picked up her drum and faded into the darkness under the trees.

Realizing she had the windowsill in a death grip, Morgan loosened her hand and pressed her forehead against the hard glass, thinking that she'd gone from arousal to terror in the space of a few minutes. The sensations weren't all that different: her heart was still pounding; a film of perspiration coated her skin; and the neck of the robe felt like it was cutting off her breath.

She opened the top two buttons, but it didn't help. The whole robe felt like it was pressing too hard against her body, making her hot and edgy.

Striding to the bathroom, she filled a glass with water and gulped it down. But it hardly helped to calm her as she thought about what had happened.

She had gone to bed in the damn robe. The same one Andre had handed her in the SUV. When she'd first put it on after the flood, she'd slipped into a dream about a woman named Linette and a man named Andre—who looked a lot like the present owner of Belle Vista.

She'd seen him clearly. But she had been inside the woman's skin, inside her head, so she didn't know what Linette looked like.

Wait! She did. She had seen the miniature portrait. The woman's hair had been long, not cropped to chin length. But her eyes had been blue, like Morgan's, and her features had been similar—as much as she could tell from a tiny oil portrait.

Something else flitted through her mind. What had Janet said? Her hair was too short. But her eyes were the right color. Did Janet know about the woman in the portrait? Had she seen it?

Morgan's pulse was pounding, and she ordered herself to calm down. She was always cool and collected in the face of danger, but since the flash flood, she'd lost her equilibrium.

She had a right to be off balance. A voodoo priestess, or someone like that, had awakened her with a malevolent chant. The woman had been outside in the shadows, working some evil spell.

Evil spell? She snorted. She didn't believe in that sort of thing. Not at all, she assured herself.

But the chanting and drumming had definitely affected her, even if the magic wasn't real. Of course, the woman certainly wanted it to be real. And for whatever reason, twice now, something strange had happened to Morgan. She'd dreamed of people she didn't know. People who seemed to have lived around here. Apparently it was only a brief ride to Belle Vista from the cabin where Linette had lived.

Morgan pulled herself up short. If there was any magic involved, it came from the damn robe. Had the voodoo priestess cursed it? Or had Andre infused it with magic?

Yeah, right.

That her mind was taking this direction appalled her. She had been hired for a specific job that had nothing to do with a voodoo priestess. Or maybe it did, come to think of it, since Andre had carefully neglected to include anything about the woman in his report on the town.

She was going to ask him about that. But not until morning when she knew where to find him.

The robe felt as if it was burning her skin, and she couldn't stand to wear it another nanosecond. Even if she had to wrap herself in a sheet, she had to get the damn thing off.

With fingers that were almost frantic, she worked the buttons, restraining the impulse to simply rip the garment down the front. When she was free of the straitjacket, she tossed it onto the small upholstered chair in the corner of the bedroom.

Naked, she breathed out a sigh of relief, then began prowling the room.

She hadn't thought to look for anything else to wear. Now she started opening drawers. In one she found a man's dress shirt, soft from many washings.

Earlier she'd shied away from the idea of wearing

anything that might belong to Andre Gascon. But necessity made her slip into the shirt. As he'd warned, it was much too long. But when she rolled up the sleeves, she decided it would make a good enough nightshirt.

Clicking the light on her watch, she saw that it was too early to get up. And she was reluctant to prowl around a strange house in the dark, dressed like a ragamuffin.

So she lay back down, knowing that the possibility of sleep was a distant one. In fact, her mind was whirling with too many ideas. She tried to think about the mystery of the chanting woman outside. But she kept coming back to the mystery of Andre Gascon. And the other man named Andre whom she had met only in two very vivid dreams.

The long-ago Andre had stirred her senses, made her aware of hot, sexy feelings that she hadn't experienced since she'd been in Trevor's arms. Dreaming of him had brought her to orgasm, if she were honest.

Damn him. He wasn't Trevor. He wasn't her husband, the love of her life. The man who had taught her about sex. Taken her skydiving and spelunking and to the Ritz in Paris. Deliberately she brought back the feelings she'd experienced when she'd learned of his death. The aching sense of loss and despair.

He had been so much a part of her life that she had hardly known how to cope. Lucky for her, her old colleague from the Peregrine Connection, Lucas Somerville, had persuaded her to join him in Baltimore. He'd gotten her a job at the Light Street Detective Agency, when she would have spent her days lying in bed in the dark, mourning her loss.

The friends she'd made at Light Street and Randolph

Security had rallied around her, too, and helped pull her through the worst of it. They were the most amazing group of men and women she had ever encountered. They had all been through dangerous and frightening experiences.

Annie Oakland and Max Dakota had almost died preventing a terrorist attack. Hunter and Kathryn Kelley had fought off a government conspiracy. Sam Lassiter had come back from an alcoholic stupor.

They were strong. They had lent her their strength. And she had told herself that if they could survive, she could, too.

Still, the reality of Trevor's loss had always been a given in her life. Even when the grief had dulled, it was still a part of her soul.

Tonight she felt more alive than she had since his death. She should welcome that feeling, she told herself. Instead she resented it. She had gotten used to living a certain way—until a dream lover had brought her to a new level of reality.

A dream lover. She hated that part of it as much as anything else. He wasn't even real.

Or was he? Did he have something to do with the present Andre Gascon? She wanted to put that notion out of her head. Maybe she did, because sometime before dawn, she fell asleep.

When she woke, bright sunlight was streaming in the window, sunlight that helped banish all the strange and disturbing notions that had been churning around in her head not so long ago.

She sat up and looked toward the door, then gave a startled exclamation.

Her suitcase and her carry-on, which had been

locked in the trunk of the car, were sitting just inside the door. Obviously, while she'd slept, someone had put them there. Janet had said Andre would get them in the morning. So had he been in her bedroom without her knowing it?

Another thought occurred to her, and she climbed quickly out of bed. The car keys had been in the ignition. Which meant that the trunk might as well have been unlocked. Anyone could have looked through her belongings before they arrived in her room. The most valuable thing she'd brought along was her computer.

Quickly she opened the zipper of the carry-on, then breathed out a sigh when she found the laptop still sitting on top of the change of clothing she always brought along on a plane in case her checked luggage was delayed. Sitting next to the carry-on was her purse, and she realized with a start that she'd forgotten all about what might be in there.

First she thumbed through her wallet. As far as she could tell, no money or credit cards were missing. Her checkbook was also in an inside pocket, along with the silver honey-bear charm Trevor had given her to tease her about her sweet tooth.

Satisfied that she hadn't been robbed, she got out toilet articles, clean underwear and a casual top and slacks, then locked the bedroom door before changing her clothing.

ANDRE STRETCHED OUT his long legs under the kitchen table, trying to appear relaxed. When Janet turned from the stove, she gave him a sympathetic look.

"It's good you got her suitcases."

"I knew she'd want her things."

"Yes."

The conversation ground to a halt. Andre fiddled with the cutlery in front of him on the table, then put down the spoon he was turning in his hand.

"You're nervous," Janet said.

"Why not? I wouldn't say we had a very calm night."

Janet nodded. "I'd like to choke Yvonne. Too bad you can't do something to shoo her away."

He sighed. "Yes, too bad she's put a protective charm around her skinny body and her blighted soul."

"She thinks her reasons for being here are valid," Janet reminded him.

"Yes," he admitted, then fell silent again. After several moments he cleared his throat. "What did you think of Morgan Kirkland?"

"She's pretty. And strong. She's not easily spooked, I think."

"Let's hope not."

He was about to say something more when the sound of footsteps in the doorway made his head jerk up, and the woman he had been waiting for stepped into the room.

Her gaze swung from him to Janet and back again. "Don't let me interrupt your conversation."

"You're not interrupting anything. Not really," he said.

MORGAN STIFLED THE URGE to fold her arms across her chest. They had been talking about her. She'd heard that much. But they'd stopped as soon as they'd become aware of her.

Well, it wasn't exactly surprising that she'd cut off the conversation. Talking about your houseguests wasn't polite. At least not in front of the guest.

Nerves had made her voice more sharp than she'd intended. It wasn't just from the conversation she'd interrupted. It was seeing Andre sitting there at the kitchen table looking so much like the Andre in the dream that she couldn't tell them apart, except for his modern clothing.

She'd been kissing the man in the dream. A lot more than kissing. He'd stroked her breasts, pulled her on top of his body, made her—

She cut off that thought. But she couldn't prevent the feelings that went with the dream. Linette had been in love with Andre, so in love that she was willing to jeopardize her future for the pleasure of making love with him.

Those weren't *her* feelings, she told herself. They belonged to another woman. She pulled herself up short. Linette wasn't real. Morgan couldn't blame Linette. The dream had come from somewhere in her subconscious. From when Andre had rescued her from the flood and held her in his arms?

Unable to move forward, she stayed where she was in the doorway. She wanted to keep her distance from Andre. She didn't want to feel anything for him or get him mixed up with the man in the dream.

"Come sit down," he said in the deep voice that was his and also the voice of the dream man from long ago.

There was no way to explain the dream—to him or to herself. So she crossed the room and pulled out a chair, being careful not to brush his knee when she sat.

"Did you sleep well, child?" Janet asked.

"Mostly," she allowed.

Holding out a cup, the housekeeper asked, "Coffee?"

"Yes, please."

The woman brought her a cup of thick black brew, rich with the smell of something she didn't usually associate with coffee.

"What kind is it?"

"A Cajun brand. With chicory. The best you'll ever taste."

Morgan took a cautious sip. It was good but strong, and she decided that despite her usual custom, cream would make a good addition. It did.

A plate of eggs and French toast sat on the table. Andre had already taken several triangles of toast. He pushed the plate toward her, a very ordinary gesture. A host offering his guest some breakfast. But sharing food took on an unintended intimacy as his strong hand brushed against hers, and a current of energy seemed to spark between them.

His voice turned deeper as he said, "Janet's eggs and *pain perdu* are excellent."

"That's the Cajun name for French toast?"

"Yes. But it's better than any you've ever tasted."

She put his bragging statement to the test and found he was right. The toast was rich and crusty, and sweet with the addition of real maple syrup.

Janet sat down at the table with them and helped herself to the toast and scrambled eggs flecked with onion and sweet red pepper. She might work for Andre, but they apparently didn't stand on ceremony.

Morgan took several bites of toast, watching the other two people at the table from under lowered lashes. The questions circling in her head were making it difficult to swallow. Finally she asked, "Who was it that I heard outside last night?"

Janet's cup clattered in the saucer.

Andre finished the bite of eggs in his mouth, then asked, "Chanting and beating a drum?"

"Yes."

His lips quirked. "Would you believe LaToya Jackson?"

"Oh, sure."

"More like the voodoo priestess," he said.

"The one who lives at the edge of town?"

"Yes."

She raised her chin. "Why didn't you tell me about her before I came here?"

He had the grace to look uncomfortable. "Is this breakfast or a business discussion?"

"Both."

"It's better for the digestion if we separate the two. We can talk about business in the office later."

Morgan wanted to press the issue. But this was his house, and she had come here to work for him. Which meant she couldn't turn everything upside down—not without a good reason. So she took some more bites of the toast and eggs while he poured himself another cup of coffee.

"Where are you from?" Janet asked.

"Harrisburg, Pennsylvania."

"How did you get into the private detective business?"

"I, uh, worked in covert operations until my husband died."

"You were married?" Janet asked in surprise.

"Yes."

Andre's expression didn't change, and she suspected he had already known that fact—and probably a lot more.

When he told Janet that the meal had been excellent, Morgan added her praise, along with a sigh of relief that they were going to get to work.

Andre led her down the hall to a small office. He walked around the desk and stood for a moment looking out a set of French doors that led to a carefully cultivated garden.

Morgan watched him making an effort to relax the tension in his shoulders. Her gaze flicked from him to the beautiful view, and a sudden insight hit her.

Stepping up behind him, she said, "You designed this garden for your own pleasure."

"Yes," he answered without turning.

"A lot of men wouldn't care about the view."

"This is my home. It's in my soul," he said.

The emotion in his voice made her chest tighten.

He sat down at the antique desk, putting the wide surface and the computer between them like a barrier.

Morgan sat in the wing chair in the corner. "You sent me a lot of material before I arrived. But you didn't give me a report on any voodoo priestess."

He sighed. "I wasn't sure the Light Street Detective Agency would take the job if I started talking about *her.*"

Chapter Five

Andre shifted in his seat. Damn the priestess. She could have given him a couple of days' grace. But she'd been right there chanting and drumming like the wicked witch of the south last night. Probably because she knew what he was up to, and she didn't want him to succeed.

Unfortunately there wasn't anything he could do about her except try to contain the damage she'd caused.

He had loved every minute of his long e-mail correspondence with Morgan. He had felt so free to tease her and joke with her and absorb every scrap of information he could pick up about her.

But he hadn't thought through the details of their day-to-day life in the armed camp where he lived. Now he was forced to give her his best imitation of an open look, as he said, "I didn't want you to think I was a nutcase. I wanted you to meet me first and see that I was…grounded. A realist. Admit it. If I'd started talking about a voodoo priestess in my e-mails, you would have decided I was a candidate for the funny farm. But if you got here and found that a…disturbed woman came to my garden at night and chanted and beat a drum, you wouldn't hold that against me."

It was Morgan's turn to look uncomfortable. "You're right."

He leaned back in his seat. "Thank you for being honest." He was having trouble concentrating. Even with the desk between them, he was too aware of her. They'd only met in person yesterday, yet it felt as if he'd known her all his life. Maybe he had.

Seeing her clinging to a tree in the middle of a raging torrent had made his heart stop. Then he'd leaped in to rescue her and held her close. He could remember the feel of her body pressed to his—even if the reason had been strictly nonsexual. That hadn't prevented him from reacting on so many different levels. Their meeting had been dramatic. Much too dramatic.

The drama hadn't ended with the rescue. After months of obsessing about her, he'd finally brought her to his house. Then he'd been forced to disappear—to spend an agonizing night wondering if she was going to pick up her suitcase and leave in the morning because the situation into which she'd stepped was just too weird for a normal person to cope with.

In the morning light she was still here, and he wanted to gather her close and hold her the way he had the day before. But he knew it would be a disaster to rush their personal relationship, so he stayed behind the desk. When he realized his fingers were clamped on the arm of the chair, he deliberately loosened them.

"Tell me about the priestess," she pressed. "What's she doing in your garden?"

"Scaring away the vampire bats."

"I'd appreciate it if you took the question seriously."

"I thought you liked my jokes."

"I did. Now I want information."

He sighed as he weighed how much to tell her. "Okay. About a hundred years ago, a young man from my family wanted to marry the niece of the local voodoo priestess. Both sets of parents forbade her to see him."

She looked startled but asked, "What happened?"

Picking his words carefully, he said, "It ended badly."

"So what are you saying—that woman comes out here to keep up an old grudge?"

"Yes. But she's just chanting and beating a drum. She's not my major problem. She's not killing people and leaving them in the swamp."

"How do you know?"

"Would she be so open about her hostility if she were?"

She nodded. "I guess not."

He used the opportunity to change the subject. "You already know two men followed you from town. You think someone at the gas station may have sabotaged your car."

"Yes."

He spread his hands. "Focus on them, not her."

"I guess I have to. But appearances can be deceiving. I met some other people, too. Like the head of the chamber of commerce, Dwight Rivers. And probably Sadie Delay. You did a good job of filling me in on the players. They seemed nice, but they didn't know I was coming out to Belle Vista."

"You're right, of course." Thinking that he shouldn't have wedged the two of them into this small room, he pushed back his chair and stood up. "We should take a look at the library and my book collection."

"Why?"

"So, if anyone comes by, it will look as though you're doing the job you told them you were hired to do."

"Is it likely that someone is going to check up on me?"

He managed a small shrug. "You never know which busybody from town is going to drop by, at least in broad daylight. And there's your car. I arranged to have it pulled out of the ditch and towed into town. Someone will bring it back here when it's finished."

She made a rather unladylike exclamation.

"What's wrong?" he asked quickly.

"I forgot all about getting the car towed. Thank you for taking care of that."

"You've had a lot on your mind since you got here."

She studied his face. "Don't tell me the car is being towed to the same gas station where I stopped?"

"That's the only alternative. I talked to the rental company, and they asked me to pay the bill, then get reimbursed from them."

"I'll do that," she said quickly. "But I hate trusting that guy Bubba to fix the brakes."

"I'll check out everything when it comes back."

"You can fix a car?"

"Yes. Out here you have to be self-sufficient. I would have done the repair work myself, but that would have meant dealing with the gas station for parts. As you can imagine, I'm trying to have as little to do with the town as possible until the situation is resolved."

"I understand," she answered.

Of course, there was no way she could really understand the whole picture yet. That would have to wait. Or maybe his plans were only a pipe dream. Before she'd arrived, he'd convinced himself that everything was going to work out the way he wanted. Now he was feeling as if the ground was slipping out from under his feet.

"Come see the library," he said, then strode out of the room.

THIS WAS THE STRANGEST JOB she'd ever accepted, Morgan thought. She'd come here on assignment for a guy who turned out to be a hunk. But that was no reason to start having erotic dreams about him as soon as they met.

She followed her host down the hall, staring at his broad shoulders, his narrow hips. In truth, she didn't want to be alone with him any longer. She wanted to escape into town. But that was impossible, with her car out of commission. Besides, she had come here to do a job, and that meant she couldn't avoid listening to anything he wanted to tell her about the case.

Because her mind was focused inward, she almost bumped into him as he stopped to open a pair of pocket doors.

When she made a small sound, he turned. "Are you all right?"

"Yes!" she snapped, then modified her tone and added, "I'm fine. I just didn't sleep too well."

"I'm sorry that you had a disturbing night," he answered as he stepped into the room beyond the doors.

Before she could stop herself, she snapped out a question. "What about your night? How was it?"

He went still. Without turning to face her, he answered, "My night was the way it always is." The way he said it was like a warning: don't go there.

She might have pressed him, but she was worried about her dreams. What if he'd had the same dream?

As that thought flashed into her head, she was glad his back was still to her.

He couldn't have had the same dream! That was impossible. And if he had, she didn't want to know about it. With her teeth clenched, she tried to force that outrageous idea out of her head.

In the next moment she had something else to focus on. The room beyond the doors took her breath away.

His office had been full of modern equipment. This room was like something she might have imagined in an old British college. It was all dark wood and floor-to-ceiling shelves with beautifully carved moldings. As she walked inside, she could smell the unmistakable aroma of old books. It was obvious that Andre had inherited a sizable collection of volumes along with the estate.

Scanning the shelves, she saw that some of the books were old and rare. But he'd obviously added to the collection, because others were modern. When she walked closer, she saw all kinds of nonfiction subjects, coffee-table books and the latest bestselling novels.

The focal point of the library was a polished stone fireplace. In front of the hearth was an almost threadbare Oriental rug, forming a conversation area for two comfortable chairs arranged to take in a view of the leaping flames. But as in Andre's office, the chairs were also positioned to look out over the beautifully tended gardens. While the office view had been restricted by high shrubs, the library windows looked out on a brick patio and a wide green lawn rimmed with flower beds.

"So, do you spend a lot of time here?" she asked.

"Yes," he said simply.

She walked over and ran her hand along some of the spines of the books. "You must haunt the bookstores in New Orleans."

"No. I used to get catalogs from various bookshops. Now I mostly order from the Internet."

"Oh."

More books were piled on a polished library table. His recent acquisitions. Or maybe they were volumes he had taken out and hadn't put back yet.

She picked up a slender book on *Fermat's Last Theorem* and flipped it open. It was full of math equations. "You understand this?"

He laughed. "Barely."

"But you find it interesting?"

"Yes."

She examined other books, amazed by the diversity. Everything from alternate energy sources to auto repair to something called *The Myth of the Werewolf.*

"Why are you reading this?" she asked.

He made a dismissive gesture with his hand. "It sounded interesting, so I bought it." Picking up another volume, *The Great Sailing Ships,* he flipped it open. "About the same level of interest as this."

"You've never seen a werewolf, have you?"

He stiffened. "That's an odd question."

"Your swamp would be the perfect place for one," she heard herself saying.

"I've never encountered one there—or a sailing ship, either."

She laughed, trying to get a handle on the man. He was a mystery. For all she knew, he had caused the problems with the town, and she had stepped into the middle of the mess he'd made. Now he was counting on her to bail him out.

She didn't want to believe that. She wanted to be on his side. Because she was attracted to him?

"What are you thinking?" he asked suddenly.

She felt her face heat. "Why do you ask?"

"You looked like you were working on an important problem."

"Just thinking about the case," she managed, then scrambled for another subject. "So you love books and gardening. How do you make a living?" It was a pretty personal question, but not out of bounds considering that she was working as a private detective for him.

It seemed he didn't mind answering. "I inherited a substantial investment portfolio. I studied the market carefully, made some good buys, diversified. I have a pretty good feel for what's going to do well and what will tank. Sometimes I make mistakes, but my picks are above average. Before the market went down a couple of years ago, I had pulled some of my money out of stocks and shifted them to bonds."

She nodded, impressed. Her own family was middle class. Her father had been a mail carrier, his government retirement his only investment. Her mom had been a grocery clerk. If Morgan hadn't won a scholarship, she probably wouldn't have gone to college. What she knew about finances would fit into a teacup, but she did have some guesses about the upkeep of a large estate.

She looked around. "Doesn't it take a considerable amount of capital to keep Belle Vista in such beautiful shape?"

"Yes, even when I do most of the work myself. I've

been tempted to sell off some of my land, but I've always been able to keep going without turning to that."

"The land is important to you?"

"It's my heritage," he said simply. He was shifting the books on the table, but his eyes were focused on the scene outside. When he drew in a strangled breath, she followed his gaze. "What?"

Without answering, he strode to the door, unlocked it and leaped outside, then hurried to a spot about halfway across the patio.

She followed him, stopping short when he squatted down to examine something.

Resting on the bricks was an object that made her breath catch. The thing looked evil—a sticky mass of tar, with stuff studding the surface. She saw orange animal hairs, seeds, blades of grass and a glass ball that looked like a marble. The whole mass was elongated, and if she squinted when she looked at it, she could see the shape of an animal. A cat?

"Did you leave this here?" she asked.

His gaze shot to her face. "You think this is mine? Why would I put something disgusting on my own patio?"

"I don't know…. To scare me?" she heard herself suggest.

"Scaring you was never my intention," he said in a strained voice. "I'm sorry you think so."

She struggled to rein in emotions that were rapidly getting out of control. "Okay, maybe somebody left it to make me wonder about your motives."

"That's a theory," he muttered. "Why would they leave it out here? This is my daily view, not yours."

"But I'm supposed to be working in the library," she

said as she gestured toward the wicked-looking thing. "What is it?"

"Gris-gris," he answered evenly, obviously making an effort to get control of himself as he took out a pocket handkerchief, picked up the blob and laid it on a table.

She stood up, too. "What exactly is gris-gris?"

"A voodoo charm."

She peered at the blob in the handkerchief. "Not a love charm, I take it," she whispered.

"Hardly."

When she reached out to touch it, his hand pulled hers back. "Leave it alone."

"Why?"

"For all I know, she could have dipped it in the toilet—or worse—before putting it here."

She snatched her hand away. "She? You think the voodoo priestess left this here?"

"Who else?"

"Somebody who wants you to think it was her. Someone else in town. A relative of the murder victims. Or one of the merchants who thinks the murders have affected business."

He sighed. "I suppose that could be an explanation."

"But you don't think so."

Anger flashed in his eyes. "I told you, people in town are afraid of me. I thought that nobody in St. Germaine except Yvonne would be brave enough to come near my house at night. Maybe that's the wrong assumption."

"Yvonne. She's the priestess?"

"Yes."

"Why is she different?"

"She's protected herself with a spell."

Morgan swiveled to face him, studying his features

to see if he was putting her on. "You believe that? I mean, you believe in voodoo? And that this woman can give herself special protections?" she added.

He waited several seconds, and she watched anger and, surprisingly, vulnerability chase themselves across his face. "I guess I have to."

While he looked so off balance, she pressed, "What does that mean?"

"It means things have happened around here that I can't explain any other way."

"Like what?"

"Like my not being able to get near her!"

"Okay," she answered, then wedged her hands on her hips, coming back to a point she'd made earlier. "You should have included that information in your report to me."

"It's not relevant. I asked you to find out who is killing people in the bayou and trying to pin it on a mysterious jaguar."

"You're sure it's not her?" she asked again.

"Yes!"

She stared out at the grounds of the estate but kept him in the edge of her vision. Apparently the subject of the voodoo priestess was an emotionally charged one for him.

"Do you think this charm can cause you harm?" she asked in a quiet voice.

He had been looking down at the gris-gris. Lifting his eyes to her, he said, "It could be meant to cause *you* harm."

His words stabbed into her, mimicking the pain that had throbbed in her head in response to the beating drum.

"Me? Why?"

"Because you're here," he said. "Because if you're living in my house, she doesn't wish you well."

She watched him carefully as she asked, "Did you do something to her? Something to make her mad?"

"Not me personally, at least as far as I know. I've stayed strictly away from her—as much as I can, anyway. But she still comes out here. It's all wound up with the grudge she holds against my family."

Morgan wanted to bombard him with more questions. But he asked quietly, "Could we drop the subject?"

"Okay," she agreed, even as she silently added, *For now.* Part of her job was judging when and how to get information. She could see it would be better to come back to the priestess when he was a little more emotionally detached.

"I'm going to get rid of this thing," he said, pointing to the charm.

"You don't mean throw it away, do you?" she asked quickly, concerned that he might be planning to destroy evidence.

"No." He laid it on the table, then said, "I'll put it in a plastic bag and save it."

She wanted to ask if he'd give it to her, but was sure he wouldn't agree, and she didn't want to make it a contest of wills. So she took a deep breath and let it out slowly before changing the subject. "I haven't checked in with my office. I should send them an e-mail and tell them I'm okay."

He seemed to visibly relax. "Do you need to use my computer?"

"I can use my laptop. But do you have two phone lines?"

"No. Just one."

"Then we'll have to figure out when I can tie up the line without getting in your way." She thought for a moment. "You don't e-mail at night, do you? I always had to wait until morning to get an answer from you."

"Right."

"So I can get online in the evening hours."

"Fine."

She stayed where she was on the patio, thinking about the question that had been hovering in her mind during the whole conversation. *Are you sorry you asked me to come here?*

That was too much of a challenge, she thought as she turned quickly back to the house.

She was too preoccupied to be watching where she was going, and when her foot caught on the edge of a brick, she started to pitch forward.

Andre moved quickly, catching her to keep her from hitting the edge of the doorway.

Neither of them spoke. He should let her go, or she should pull away. But the only move either of them made was for his arms to tighten around her and pull her closer.

She stayed where she was, lowering her head against his shoulder. "I wasn't watching where I was going," she whispered.

"Are you all right?"

"Yes," she murmured. Secretly, she had wondered how she would react to being held by the real man again after the intensity of her experience with the dream lover. The depth of her feelings shocked her.

As he cradled her in his arms, it seemed she had lost the will to act sensibly, at least for the moment. When she raised her head, he looked down at her, the question in his eyes as clear as if he had spoken to her in words.

And she answered with her eyes, because words were beyond her at the moment.

Slowly, giving her time to change her mind, he lowered his mouth to hers. Maybe he intended the kiss to be gentle. It did start out sweet, even tender. But it took only seconds for it to change from sweet to sweltering.

Something happened. Something she couldn't explain. She was back in the dream, yet not the dream. They were Andre and Linette.

No, Andre and Morgan. Andre and Linette. Andre and Morgan. She didn't know who she was anymore.

The only thing she understood for sure was that she was engulfed by the sensation of his lips moving urgently against hers, his hands gliding up and down her back, the rich scent of his body.

The kiss melted her bones, made her cling to him to stay erect. Whoever she was—whoever they were—this man spoke to her in a primitive language well below any verbal level. But they both understood it.

When his tongue stroked along the seam of her lips, she opened for him, welcoming the more intimate contact that brought with it the essence of man and a hint of the maple syrup he'd eaten at breakfast. The taste of him was familiar to her. As his tongue explored the inside of her lips, her teeth, she was sure that she had done this with him before.

No, not with him. In the dream.

She was still coping with confusion, but as he deepened the kiss, she felt the erotic sensation travel downward through her body, making her nipples tighten and her sex turn liquid.

How many months had it been before Linette had dared to let Andre kiss her this way?

How long before Linette had realized that she would make love with Andre, whether a priest had blessed their union or not?

Perhaps the directness of that thought was what brought her back to reality. Her hands shifted from this Andre's neck to his shoulders, pushing him away instead of clinging, and somehow she managed to get out one coherent syllable, "No."

Chapter Six

Andre's response was instantaneous. He let go of the woman in his arms, then took a step back, suddenly embarrassed on several different levels—starting with the erection that must certainly be standing out like a shovel handle against the fly of his slacks. Somehow he resisted the urge to look down at his front as he thought about the slew of mistakes he had made in the past few minutes. He should never have gathered Morgan into his arms in the first place. And he should never have let her response to him unleash his own greed.

He was a disciplined man—as disciplined as he could be, given the hand that fate had dealt him. But once he'd folded her against himself, everything he'd known about discipline had fled his mind.

"I'm sorry," he said.

She took a step back, and he saw she was doing the same thing he was—struggling to compose herself.

When she spoke, her voice was high and shaky. "There's no point in assigning blame to either one of us." She stopped and cleared her throat. "The point is, we have to work together. I have to live here. We need to keep things on a professional level."

"Yes," he agreed, relieved that she wasn't telling him she was going to call a cab and bail out.

She was speaking again, and he tried to focus on the words through the humming in his brain. "Then I'll go off and e-mail my office and let them know that I'm on the job."

"Okay," he agreed quickly, because now that she had broken the hot, desperate kiss, he needed to be alone.

He waited for her to turn and leave. Instead she said, "And I need to think about why you're having trouble giving me complete answers to my questions."

Probably she'd thrown that at him to cover her embarrassment before she made her hasty exit.

With a jerky motion, he took several steps toward the serenity of the garden. The landscape he'd created always soothed him. Not today. He had cooked up a reason for asking her to come here and work for him. Well, not exactly cooked up. What he'd told her was true, as far as it went. Unfortunately, she wasn't taking his explanations at face value. She kept digging for more information. Information he wasn't willing to spit out.

With a muttered curse, he closed his eyes. He didn't want to think about answering her pointed questions. He wanted to think about the kiss. To relive every tantalizing detail.

Yes. The kiss. That was easier.

Morgan might have ended it, but while it had lasted, it had been glorious.

He'd felt an instant connection to her. It must have been the same for her, judging from the heat they'd generated.

He sighed, leaning more firmly against the French door because his legs felt unsteady.

He thought about how her lips had felt against his. Her tongue. Her breasts pressed to his chest.

When he started getting hard again, he made a rough noise, then struggled to cut off the sensations assaulting his body. The intimate contact had made his head spin. It had been a mistake, and he'd better keep his hands off her until they got to know each other better. Then maybe he'd have the guts to tell her the real reason why he'd hired her.

He stifled a sharp laugh. Or maybe not. It had seemed like a great idea at the time. Now he couldn't help thinking he'd been kidding himself all along when he'd asked her here.

Pushing away from the door, he headed down the hall to his office and closed the door. The computer was already on, and all he had to do was touch the mouse to make the screen spring to life. He might have gone onto the Web, but he remembered that Morgan needed the phone line.

So he decided to spend a few hours checking his credit card records that he'd downloaded earlier. That should cool him off pretty well.

He had every intention of checking his bank statement. Instead he opened the Morgan Kirkland file and began reading over all the information he'd collected on her.

Morgan Kirkland, age thirty. Marital status: widow. He didn't like that part. He would have preferred her to have been unmarried. But he wasn't old-fashioned enough to think she needed to be a virgin. Besides, he didn't have his choice about that or anything else.

He'd started looking up information on private investigators seven months ago then rejected each one. But the moment he'd found the Light Street Detective Agency, something had felt different. Eagerly, he'd accessed their staff of agents. As soon as he'd read the name Morgan Kirkland, he'd known she was the right one.

She wasn't pictured, of course. None of the agents had been, since they often worked undercover. But he had excellent Web skills, and he'd traced her back to her yearbook photo at Penn State. Seeing her picture had made his chest go suddenly tight. When he'd gotten his breath back, he'd booted up his special photographic program and added twelve years to her face.

He stared at that picture now, thinking that the real woman was more complicated than the manufactured image.

Quirking his lips, he went back to her résumé. It fudged her background, but he'd put several sources of information together and come to the conclusion that she'd worked for a super-secret government organization called the Peregrine Connection. There was no direct information on Peregrine, beyond speculation as to whether it actually existed. But he gathered that both she and her dead husband, Trevor Kirkland, had been covert agents for them. They'd met in college where he'd studied international relations and she'd majored in law enforcement. Without going into detail, her résumé said she'd worked undercover both in and out of the U.S.

Then the husband had been killed, and Light Street had scooped her up. Probably because she had friends who already worked for them or the staff of their sister organization, Randolph Security.

Since coming onboard, she'd demonstrated extraordinary bravery and excellent investigative skills. But that wasn't why he had hired her.

Instead he'd sensed that she was the woman who could get him out of the trap he'd been sucked into—through no fault of his own, he told himself firmly.

He switched files, to their e-mail correspondence. He'd read it so many times that he'd memorized almost every sentence. They'd started off discussing business, but incidents from their daily lives had crept into the conversation. He remembered the confession she'd made about buying a very expensive leather jacket. He'd reassured her that there was nothing wrong with indulging herself.

He remembered when she'd told him about an all-Beethoven program she'd enjoyed at the concert hall in Baltimore. He'd wished he could have been there. For the Beethoven and her company.

Their relationship had blossomed over the past few weeks. He'd enjoyed the give and take with her, enjoyed the way she'd opened up with him. He'd even ended up advising her how to fix a leaky faucet in her Baltimore town house.

Now he kept wondering if bringing Morgan here and not telling her the whole story made him as guilty as his grandfather.

MORGAN HURRIED UPSTAIRS, hoping that she wouldn't bump into Janet because she was sure her face would give away her recent activity.

Her response to Andre had been supercharged. She didn't like that for a lot of different reasons. She had told herself nobody could take her husband's place in her bed—or in her life. But she had certainly forgotten about Trevor in Andre Gascon's arms. She was being disloyal to a memory that should have been sacred.

Clenching her teeth, she strode into her room and closed the door. After unplugging the phone on the nightstand, she settled on the bed and connected to the Internet.

Then she quickly sent a message to Light Street, telling them that she had arrived safely. She debated what else to add and finally mentioned that men in town had exhibited hostility when she'd asked for directions to Belle Vista. She also noted that Andre Gascon seemed to be less than forthcoming in his answers to her questions about the presumed voodoo priestess who had been outside her window chanting the night before. But she also credited him with rescuing her from a flash flood, omitting any details that might alarm her friends back home.

A little smile flickered on her lips as she thought about their reaction to the voodoo part. Probably that would give them pause, but they knew she could handle herself—if they didn't think she'd lost her mind.

Of course, as far as she was concerned, a more urgent problem was not having a weapon. Her Glock had been swept away by the flood. Although she knew from her research that there was a gun shop in town where she could replace it, that would have to wait until she got her car back from the garage and Andre checked it out for her.

Turning off her computer, she strode to the window. The view looked different in the daylight, of course, but she was pretty sure she could pick out the tree where she'd seen the woman last night. After stuffing some plastic bags and thin rubber gloves into her pocket, she headed downstairs again. On the first floor, she explored until she found a back door off the same hallway that led to the kitchen.

Outside, she breathed in the damp air, then looked down at the garden from the vantage point of the landing. The grounds had impressed her the evening before, although she'd hardly gotten to enjoy the view before Andre had hustled her into the house. In the bright sunlight, the garden was stunning, with carefully mulched beds almost devoid of weeds.

Descending the steps, she wandered among the flower beds. When she came to a blade of grass that obviously didn't belong among the begonias, she pulled it up, then wondered where she was going to get rid of it.

As she walked across the broad lawn and away from the house, she could see that Andre had different garden beds scattered around the lawn. Many were edged with bright annuals to provide continuous color. In the center were grouped perennials like irises, peonies or lilies that would provide varying bursts of color throughout the year.

The garden—and the house—said a lot about the owner of Belle Vista. He was supremely self-sufficient. He made long-range plans. He loved living in a beautiful setting. He was willing to work hard to achieve his goals.

At the margins of the garden, Andre had cultivated informal groups of natural plants. Under a live oak, just past a patch of spearlike ferns, Morgan found a rough circle of trampled earth. As she examined the spot, a shiver traveled over her skin, despite the heat. This must be where the voodoo priestess had been standing, although she saw no evidence beyond the trampled ground.

How often did the woman come here? Was her visit a special treat for Andre's librarian, along with the gris-gris?

Morgan glanced back over her shoulder. Without her gun for protection, she wanted to keep the house in sight. But she also wanted to do some more investigating, so she began walking back and forth, checking the ground. About fifteen yards from the edge of the manicured area, she spotted something white among the leaves covering the ground. When she squatted down, she found several cigarette butts. Pulling on a rubber glove, she picked up the butts and shoved them into a plastic bag. Methodically, she looked for more evidence but found nothing besides bird droppings. The butts would have DNA evidence from saliva. But there was a good chance the rain had washed it away. Still, she was going to send the evidence to Light Street for analysis.

The hair prickled on the back of her neck, and she looked quickly over her shoulder, expecting to find Andre staring at her. She saw no one. Yet the feeling of being watched persisted.

Before she'd come here, Andre had told her which books to read about the natural environment. Now she pretended great interest in a giant hooded pitcher plant as she scanned the underbrush around her. Although nothing stirred, the feeling of uneasiness persisted. The house was out of sight now, but she knew the way back because bright sunlight marked the edge of the lawn.

Still, she kept her ears tuned for danger. When she heard something moving in the underbrush, she went stock-still, visions of jaguars playing through her head.

With part of her mind, she knew she was out to prove to herself that Morgan Kirkland hadn't changed since coming to Belle Vista and meeting Andre Gascon. She still had the same reckless disregard for her own safety.

But she had enough sense to hesitate for several minutes, stepping farther into the shadows, moving cautiously from tree trunk to tree trunk. It was a secret relief to find she could only walk another twenty yards before she came to the bank of what she would have called a small lazy river, although she suspected the people down here would refer to it as a bayou.

She followed its course for another couple of hundred yards, moving farther from the house, farther from safety, until she came to a place where she could see an island about six feet from shore, with a fallen log lying across the banks, providing access. The log was about three feet above the water, the near end resting on a bed of sphagnum moss. It was too narrow to be a good bridge, but when she moved closer, she saw muddy footprints in the moss and on the log top, suggesting that someone had crossed over. Someone with a secret to hide out here in the swamp?

It could be Andre. But what if it wasn't him? What if someone else was hiding an illegal operation on his property and wanted everyone to keep out of the area? A murderous jaguar would certainly discourage trespassers.

She stared across at the tangle of vegetation on the island, trying to figure out if someone had been over there recently, or on a regular basis. Some of the saw palmettos and pond spice bushes looked trampled. But she couldn't be sure if a person or an animal had done it.

The place seemed ordinary, yet it gave her a creepy feeling, as though something lurked on the other side of the log, waiting to grab her.

Nonsense, she told herself firmly.

CROUCHING IN THE SHADOWS, the watcher on the island stayed very still—still as the nearest tree trunk.

Morgan Kirkland was standing on the bank, staring across the brown water, looking as if she wanted to find out what was going on over here.

"Come on. Come on and try it. But watch out for the booby trap and the gators."

She'd come marching out of the house this morning and started poking around. Then she'd picked up something from the ground and put it in a plastic bag.

The bitch was much too nosy. In town she had given out the story that she was a librarian. If so, why was she poking around out here in the bayou? Why was she so damn interested in the island?

"Come on," the watcher whispered again. "You want to cross? You've got to do it just right or you'll give my pet gator a nice breakfast treat. Usually he has to make do with the chunks of meat I feed him. But maybe not today." It was hard to suppress a chuckle, but the watcher managed.

That image of Ms. Kirkland flailing around in the water, getting dragged down to the muddy bottom, was comforting. Little Miss Librarian—if that's what she really was—didn't know what she'd gotten into when she'd taken a job with Andre Gascon. She couldn't imagine the dangers lurking in the bayou surrounding his nice green lawn and that house he was so proud of.

Was she dumb enough to come out of the house at

night? Maybe there was some way to lure her out here so the sheriff could find her in the morning—clawed to death.

That would serve her right for sticking her nose where it didn't belong.

ONCE AGAIN Morgan tried to shake off the creepy feeling that she wasn't alone out here. Turning in all directions, she searched the underbrush but saw nothing. She should go back, but maybe she could make a quick trip to the island first.

As she stepped up onto the makeshift bridge, she looked down at the brown water and froze. A smaller fallen log floated near the bank, only it didn't look quite right. The observation was confirmed when it raised an elongated head, gave her what looked like a hopeful glance and then opened a mouth full of sharp teeth.

Instinctively she jumped back onto the muddy ground. That was no log. It was an alligator, waiting for someone to fall—or get pushed—into the water.

Nervously she looked back over her shoulder, suddenly aware that she'd come pretty far into the swamp, far enough to lose sight of the place where the wilderness ended and the garden began.

Damn! She wanted a replacement for her gun. And maybe a compass. She didn't know this part of the country, and the green-and-brown landscape gave no clue to her location.

"Stupid," she muttered. But she did know one thing. She had come along the bayou, and when she looked down at the ground, she could see her footprints in the mud.

Feeling as if she'd made a very fortunate escape, she followed her own trail back along the bank, then found the spot where her footprints veered off toward the house.

Quickly she hurried toward the gardens, then stopped short when she spotted Andre standing near the edge of the trees, his hands wedged on his hips. His face was grim, but she forced herself to walk directly toward him, then stopped several feet away.

What was he angry about, exactly? Had he spotted her near the island and been worried that she'd find something he wanted to keep hidden?

He bolstered her suspicion with his clipped remark. "I don't want you tramping around outside the garden area by yourself."

"Why not?"

"It's dangerous!"

For you or me? she wanted to ask, but she kept her own counsel.

"What were you doing out there?"

"Looking for evidence," she answered immediately.

"Of what?"

She raised her chin. "I found the spot where the voodoo priestess was standing last night."

"I know where she was!" he snapped.

"And do you know who else has been out there in the underbrush?"

He stiffened. "Nobody!"

"You're wrong. Unless she smokes cigarettes." Holding up the plastic bag, she displayed what she'd found earlier.

As he stared at the contents, his eyes widened. "Where did those come from?"

"Not too far from where the priestess had been standing."

"That explains it," he muttered.

"Explains what?"

"Why I didn't find them."

She regarded him steadily. "What does she have to do with it?"

For a moment he looked like a boy who had been caught telling lies. Then his mouth firmed. "I told you, she's given herself a protective charm. So I stay away from the area where she's been, which is why I didn't see that stuff."

"And what exactly does the charm do to you?"

He glared at her. "If I get close to her, or where she's been, my throat closes up. Like someone with anaphylactic shock."

She made a strangled sound. "Really?"

"Yeah, really!"

He walked closer and inspected the plastic bag in her hand. "Too bad whoever left these didn't drop a set of keys or a wallet."

The sound of a car in the driveway made them both turn. From the side of the house where they stood, she could see a black-and-white patrol car rolling to a stop.

As a tall, solidly built man climbed out, Andre cursed under his breath. "Sheriff Marlon Jarvis has thought of an excuse to pay us a call."

"Old Razorback," she said, recalling the name Andre had given the lawman.

He laughed. "Don't let him hear you say that."

She watched Andre deliberately relax his shoulders, then stiffen again as he looked toward the plastic bag she held. *Merde.*

"What now?"

"If he sees that and figures it's significant, he'll confiscate it."

"Not to worry." Morgan took a step to the side, then lowered her arm along her leg, letting the bag slip to the ground behind a gnarled trunk.

"Thank you," Andre murmured.

"No problem."

Silently they started in the direction of the drive.

The sheriff stood on the blacktop, staring toward them. He looked like a classic example of a small-town lawman, with a blue uniform, high trooper boots and a broad-brimmed hat. As they drew closer, she saw that his face was broad and ruddy, his features a bit coarse. Probably he was in his late forties or early fifties. The extra flesh on his frame and the tense way he stood told her where Andre had gotten the nickname.

"Afternoon," he said in an even voice. Then, addressing Morgan, he said, "I'm Sheriff Jarvis."

"Morgan Kirkland," she supplied without offering her hand.

"Afternoon," Andre said, using the same noncommittal tone as Jarvis. "To what do we owe this pleasure?" he asked, although they all knew that the encounter wasn't likely to be enjoyable.

"Just making sure everything is okay."

"Everything is fine," Andre clipped out.

Jarvis turned to Morgan. "You stopped in town yesterday afternoon and asked directions to Belle Vista, Miss Kirkland."

"Mrs.," she corrected immediately.

He looked surprised.

"My husband was killed in Afghanistan."

"Oh. I'm sorry."

"It was several years ago," she answered, knowing her loss was a good way to make most people uncomfortable.

She could tell she had succeeded with Old Razorback. But she also knew he wasn't going away until he was good and ready. He waited a beat before saying, "Your car was towed back to town this morning. The driver said there was evidence of a flash flood on the road."

"Yes, there was. It was lucky that Mr. Gascon was worried when I didn't show up on time and came looking for me," she said, unconsciously drawing closer to him.

"Yes, lucky," the sheriff repeated as though he was taking her assessment under advisement.

She thought about mentioning the two men who had followed her. But they would just bring up the issue of the jaguar that had scared them off, and she sensed that getting into a discussion about the cat would be a bad idea. Probably, at this point, the less she said to this man, the better. Still, she couldn't stop herself from asking, "Did you get a report on my car?"

"No."

"Something was wrong with the brakes. I was having trouble controlling the vehicle. I thought it strange that it happened not long after I stopped at the service station in town."

"Are you implying something?" he asked.

"Not at all," she said evenly.

"Funny thing about that flash flood," he said. "Your car was found on the side nearest town. How did you get across?"

She might have asked if he thought she'd flown over the water on a broomstick. Instead she said, "I was looking for ferns or something to put under my wheels to get me out of the ditch, so I was out of the car when the water suddenly swept over the road. Mr. Gascon fished me out."

The sheriff whistled through his teeth as he eyed Andre. "I guess she *was* lucky you came along."

"Mmm-hmm," Andre answered evenly.

The lawman turned back to her, switching topics abruptly. "I understand you're going to be working in the library here."

"I've already started. And I should be getting back now," she said, taking a step away. With anyone else, her tone and body language would have ended the discussion. Apparently the sheriff wasn't finished with her.

"Just a minute. I assume Mr. Gascon has told you about the problems we've been having around here."

She felt her stomach knot, but she kept her expression bland. "I'm a researcher. I did a lot of reading about the area before agreeing to take the job."

"And you're not worried about working out at Belle Vista in such an isolated location?"

"Are you trying to get me to quit?" she demanded.

"No. I'm making sure you understand the consequences of living here."

Beside her, Andre looked as though he was going to punch the guy out—a very bad idea when it came to a cop. She wanted to put a restraining hand on his arm, but that would imply a level of intimacy that would seem strange to an outsider. It seemed strange to her, actually. Instead she said, "I've been taking care of myself for a long time. I can take care of myself here. But I do have a question about the area."

"Yes?"

"I saw a sign for a voodoo priestess in a house at the edge of town."

"That would be Miss Sonnier."

Sonnier. The same name as the woman in the dream.

"She supports herself with her voodoo activities?"

Both Andre and the sheriff looked uncomfortable.

"Why do you ask?" Jarvis drawled.

"If she's any good, I might want a consultation."

"I wouldn't recommend it," he shot back.

"Why not?"

"There's been bad blood between her family and the Gascons for generations. If you're associated with the estate, she won't be friendly to you."

"Well, I appreciate your filling me in on town politics," she said.

"I wouldn't exactly call it politics."

"How would you phrase it?"

"Like I said, bad blood."

"The Hatfields and the McCoys? Do the Sonniers and the Gascons shoot each other?"

"It hasn't come to that," Jarvis muttered. Taking out a business card, he handed it to her. "If you have any problems, give me a call."

"I certainly will."

When he climbed into his car and drove away, she and Andre both sighed with relief.

"Nice guy." Morgan smirked. "Has his family been here for generations, too?"

"As a matter of fact, no. He came to St. Germaine when the town was looking to upgrade its police force.

He's well trained, but I guess he bought into the stories he heard about me."

She nodded, because she had to agree.

"You were good at handling him," Andre said.

"I've had experience with men like him."

"Which is?"

"Suspicious. Eager to pin something on you. Guys who get off on being an authority figure so they can throw their weight around." She sighed. "And men who think they're better than any woman."

"A good description." He looked up and apparently saw that the sun was low in the western sky. "We generally have an early dinner around six at this time of year."

"And then," she asked, hearing the edge in her voice, "you're going to disappear and be unavailable, the way you were last night?"

Chapter Seven

"Yes," Andre clipped out. "That's a given."

Morgan kept her gaze on his face. "And another one of the factors that you forgot to mention when you hired me for this job."

His features closed up. "Sorry. Maybe you should take the sheriff's advice and leave."

"Don't tempt me," she retorted.

While they'd been talking to Jarvis, she'd felt herself and Andre drawing closer, forming a solid front in the face of the lawman's hostility. The feeling of connection had snapped again, replaced with mistrust.

She wasn't sure what to say. Apparently, neither was he. After several seconds of silence, he turned and started back across the lawn.

She thought he was going into the house, but he veered off toward a clump of azalea bushes.

He hadn't invited her to follow, but she did anyway, curious about where he was headed.

When she got closer, she saw that the large azaleas hid a garden shed, painted green and brown to blend in with the landscape.

He took out a key and unlocked a padlock holding

the door closed. She stopped just outside, regarding the interior and marveling. The walls were covered with pegboard on which garden tools were hung with military precision. She shook her head as she compared his system to the jumble inside her own garage, and she shuddered when she thought about what he'd say about the junk piled in her spare room.

"What?" he demanded.

"You're neat and organized."

"That's bad?"

"It's admirable."

"It makes life easier."

As she watched, he got down several sizes of clippers and a pair of gardening gloves, which he placed in a wheelbarrow.

"What are you doing?" she asked.

"I'm going to trim some of the bushes."

"Why?"

"Because I try to do some work in the garden every day. That way, nothing gets out of hand."

Methodical again. Stepping aside, she watched him steer the wheelbarrow toward the edge of the lawn, and debated whether to follow.

She doubted she was going to get any more information out of him at the moment, unless it was about plants and flowers. So she said, "I'll see you at dinner," and headed back to the house.

ANDRE WATCHED Morgan depart, then waited to make sure she wasn't going to change her mind and come back.

When he was sure he was alone, he wheeled the equipment across the lawn and under the trees. He'd made a hedge of wild roses to keep animals and people out of his private garden, but he knew how to weave his way past the thorns. Inside were beds where he cultivated plants he'd found in the bayou and brought to a spot near the house.

He always felt a little anxious when he approached this place. The low-growing plants with their curly red-edged leaves had assumed a frightening importance in his life. Once, when the temperature had dropped below freezing, his entire supply had been wiped out. He'd had to comb the bayou for more and he'd been in a panic until he'd found them.

Now Morgan's bag of cigarette butts had him worried that someone might stumble in here. With a grimace, he squatted down, inspecting his stock. They were doing well, including the new transplants.

He snipped some yellowing foliage off one of the mature specimens, then cut several new green leaves. Lifting them to his face, he drank in the familiar, earthy aroma. An aroma he knew had invaded the pores of his body.

Later he would take them back to the small lab in his bathroom and cook them, making sure his supply of the tea he made from them didn't run out.

For now he tucked the clippings into a small bag. Then he headed back to the manicured area near the house, where his father had planted a bank of forsythia. They grew like weeds, and the only way he could keep them in check was to cut them back every few months.

He worked steadily, selecting canes that could be thinned and clipping off runners that had crept out from the mature plants. Most of those were rooted, and he hated to throw them away. But he'd learned that an orderly garden meant a ruthless gardener.

He kept his focus on the work and managed not to think about Sheriff Jarvis. Morgan, however, kept creeping back into his mind.

He had thought he knew what to expect when he contacted the Light Street Detective Agency and asked specifically for Morgan Kirkland. He hadn't known that she wasn't great at following directions. She made her own decisions, sometimes too impulsively—like tramping off into the bayou.

His heart had stopped when he'd seen her come out from under the trees and known that she could have gotten into big trouble.

He wasn't used to dealing with someone like her. In truth, he wasn't used to dealing with anyone besides Janet on a daily basis.

Probably he was too set in his ways. And unrealistic.

In the face of conflict, his natural tendency had always been to withdraw. Like when the kids at school had teased him about his weird old man.

At the moment he was thinking about telling Janet that he wouldn't be coming down to dinner. Then he reminded himself that avoiding Morgan would be a mistake, even when she made him uncomfortable. He needed to get to know her better. Hiding in his room wasn't the way to do that, so he dumped the forsythia canes in the compost pile, methodically put his tools away and went in to start brewing his special tea. Then he'd take a shower and change his clothing.

MORGAN HAD NEVER FELT comfortable being waited on, so she arrived in the kitchen a little early and asked what she could do to help Janet get the meal ready.

The housekeeper pointed her toward the drawers where the silverware was kept, and she was setting the table when Andre came into the kitchen. She'd been listening for him, but somehow he'd sneaked up on her, silent as a cat. Her hand shook, and she dropped a fork on the table, hearing the clatter above the sound of Janet's final dinner preparations.

"I'll wear lumberjack boots next time," he said, sounding as if he was trying to sound playful.

"No harm done," Morgan answered in the same tone.

He'd dressed for dinner in a crisp dress shirt and dark slacks. She was glad she'd changed into a simple knit dress and sandals.

Turning away from Andre, she found Janet watching them. Caught staring, the housekeeper quickly whirled back to the stove. But she hadn't hidden her interest.

What was her stake in this? Probably she wanted Andre to solve his problems. Probably she was wondering if Morgan was the right person for the job, and she hadn't made up her mind yet.

Meanwhile, she made a good buffer between the other two diners.

When they were all seated and had served themselves, they ate in silence, until Janet jumped in with a question, the way she had at breakfast.

"So where do you live in Baltimore?"

"I have a town house in Fells Point. Near the water," she added. "If I'm in the mood for some exercise, I can walk to work."

Changing the subject, she tipped her head toward Andre. "Your turn. Where did you go to school?"

"If you mean kindergarten through high school—in St. Germaine."

"What about college?"

He shifted in his chair. "I didn't go beyond high school."

She struggled to hide her surprise, but it apparently showed on her face.

"I was needed at home. My father was sick, and I had to run the estate."

"At eighteen?"

"Yes."

"But you're obviously very intelligent. You're interested in a lot of subjects. You should have gone on with your schooling." Realizing that that probably sounded condescending, she closed her mouth before she could stick her foot in any farther.

"You don't have to go to college to be well read. That's one of the reasons I have so many books. If a subject draws me, I read about it."

Morgan nodded.

"You ought to have seen him when he was three," Janet chimed in. "He taught himself to read. He'd come to me with a book and point to a word and say, 'Does that say yellow?' or 'Does that say neighborhood?' And it would. He picked up reading with a little help from me. When he was eight, he sent away for a kit and built a color TV because his father wouldn't buy one."

A look flashed between Andre and the housekeeper, and Morgan could see that their relationship was strong.

"You helped his mother take care of him?" she asked.

The woman's features contorted. "His mother left," she said.

"Janet raised me," Andre said gently.

"What about your father?"

"He was usually holed up in the library."

Morgan was about to ask another question when Andre glanced up. As he looked toward the window, the blood drained from his face.

"What?" she asked, wondering what he'd seen.

"I forgot the time," he said, his deep voice turning hollow.

"It's cloudy out," Janet answered. "That's why it's so dark."

"Maybe," he muttered. Shoving back his chair, he bolted from the room. Moments later she heard the back door slam.

Morgan pushed her chair away from the table and started to follow him. Janet jumped up and grabbed her arm. "Let him go."

"Where?"

The woman gave her a fierce look, then made an effort to relax her features. "Out," she said, making it clear that she wasn't going to answer any more questions about Andre's strange behavior.

Snatching his plate from the table, she carried it to the counter, covered it with plastic wrap and stuck it in the refrigerator.

Morgan wavered for a minute. "It's been a long day. I think I'll go up. Thank you for a delicious dinner."

"You don't have to leave just because he did."

She debated staying in the kitchen and trying some other question on the housekeeper, but she had the feeling she'd be wasting her time since both of them were now on edge. Instead she repeated her thanks, then left the room and headed for the stairs. Before she got there, she changed her mind and went back to the library. Switching on the lights, she scanned the shelves, amazed all over again by the wide variety of subjects, especially now that she knew that Andre's higher education had come from this library.

He ran an estate, managed his investments, did his own gardening, landscaping and home remodeling.

Unconsciously she found herself comparing him to her husband. Trevor had been obsessed with his job. Most of their conversations had been about their assignments.

Andre seemed to be the complete opposite. He was all caught up in what DIY shows might call "nesting." A lot of women would consider him an excellent catch—except that there was something strange about him. He had secrets. And he kept disappearing at inopportune times.

Why? Was he a drunk or a drug addict? Was that where he went at night—to drink himself into a stupor or drown his pain in chemical remedies?

Suddenly she remembered a conversation she'd once had with the mother of a friend who worked in a nursing home. There were some old people she'd called— What was it? Morgan thought for a minute. Sundowners. That was the term for the residents who seemed okay during the day but wigged out as soon as the sun went down. She didn't know why that was true. Could it apply to someone Andre's age?

She clenched and unclenched her fists, hating the way her thoughts were branching off into strange speculation. If Andre had only been honest with her, she could stop making up answers to the questions spinning around in her head. He'd gotten her to trust him enough to come down here. Now she was wondering if she should have been more cautious.

She was angry by the time she reached the top of the

stairs. The thought crossed her mind that maybe she should stroll down the hall and start opening doors. She could find his room and wait for him to come back. But that would be a clear invasion of his privacy. She wasn't going to do that until she had exhausted other means of getting the information she needed to make sensible opinions about him.

Instead she walked slowly to her own room, stepped inside and closed the door. Without turning on the light, she crossed the floor and looked out the window, her gaze searching the area under the trees where the voodoo priestess had put on her show the night before.

As far as Morgan could see, no one was there, and she breathed out a little sigh. Then a flash of movement caught her eye. Something stirred in the shadows fifty yards from where the woman had been standing the night before. She couldn't tell what, but it didn't look like a man. Or if it was a man, he was on his hands and knees.

She leaned toward the window, trying to get a better look, but the darkness under the trees frustrated her efforts to figure out what she was seeing. Then the thing moved closer. She saw a large elongated head, pointed ears, a low, lithe body covered with orange fur and black spots.

As the animal moved along the edge of the open area, its image solidified into a shape she had seen before, and a strangled sound rose in her throat.

It was a jaguar. The same one she had seen on the road—or his cousin.

Then it had been out in the wild. Now it was right here—at Belle Vista.

The closed window and fifty yards separated her

from the animal. But its hearing must have been excellent. It raised its head, the yellow eyes instantly finding and pinning her. Her breath caught in her throat as the animal stared at her and she stared back.

The mottled tail lashed back and forth, the way a house cat would signal its anger. But this was no little tabby. This was a wild animal with claws and teeth that could rip a person's skin to shreds.

As the cat stared directly at her, goose bumps rose on her skin. For heartbeats she and the animal stood facing each other as though there were some kind of supernatural connection between them. Then the jaguar took a step back, and another.

She had been frightened. Now she had to stifle the need to open the window and tell him to wait.

It was a strange impulse. A dangerous impulse. Yet she felt a deep sense of loss as the cat disappeared into the shadows, leaving her alone at the window.

She stood there for several minutes. In the darkness, the jaguar howled—a long, lonely sound that pierced her like a sharp blade.

Quickly she reached up and pulled the curtains closed. He couldn't see her now. And neither could the voodoo priestess.

With deliberate steps, she crossed to the night table and turned on the light. The warm glow was comforting.

Now that she was alone, she couldn't help wondering if the jaguar had been real or if she had made him up.

She didn't know, but suddenly she felt cold all over. In the bathroom she turned on the shower, waited until the water heated, then stepped under the hot spray, letting it pound against her back and shoulders, soothing her jangled nerves.

After drying off, she went to bed.

To her relief she fell asleep quickly and slept undisturbed till morning.

FULL OF RENEWED ENERGY, she changed into jeans and a T-shirt and went downstairs. When she walked into the kitchen, Janet looked up. "Andre asked me to tell you he won't be available today."

Suddenly deflated, Morgan demanded, "Where is he?"

"He left early to go get some supplies."

"In St. Germaine?"

"No. He needed some things he could only get in New Orleans."

"He could have asked if I wanted to go with him," she snapped.

"He wanted to get an early start and you were still sleeping."

Morgan struggled not to take out her frustration on Janet. Instead she ate a quick breakfast, then cleared her throat. "Can I borrow a knife?"

"For what?"

"I feel funny poking around in the swamp without any protection."

"You shouldn't be poking around in the bayou at all!"

"It's part of my job," she murmured.

Janet sighed and gestured toward one of the kitchen drawers. Opening it, she took a medium-size knife, then exited the kitchen, holding the weapon down beside her leg as she stepped outside and descended the steps.

Heading for the trees, she was sure that Janet was watching her. But she refused to look around to find out for sure.

She had seen the cat under an oak tree. When she reached it, she stopped and couldn't hold back a curse. Someone had raked the dirt, obliterating any chance of finding the prints.

Her jaw set in a determined line, she began walking in a circle, her eyes fixed on the ground, widening the circle every time she came back to a spot opposite the lawn where she'd started. It took her ten repetitions, but she finally found the tracks, leading away into a stand of small pines.

So the cat hadn't been her imagination!

Well, that was something, anyway. She was already pretty far into the swampy area. She glanced over her shoulder, thinking she should go back to the house. Instead she deliberately went in the opposite direction, toward the bayou. Before she reached the island, she used the knife to cut off a sapling, then stripped off the small branches. If the water wasn't too deep, she could use the pole to steady herself as she walked across the log.

With the pole in one hand, she walked along the bank, searching for the island. It materialized out of the shadows several minutes later, looking dark and menacing. But she was pretty sure she was projecting her mood onto the place. It was just a patch of ground like any other.

Before she could change her mind, she stepped up on the log and probed at the mud. As she had hoped, the water was only a couple of feet deep.

Feeling more confident, she took another step, then moved the pole, taking each step slowly and carefully.

She was a quarter of the way across the log when the pole sank into thick muck, throwing her off balance. Her feet slipped on the treacherous surface, and she dropped the stick, pinwheeling her arms to keep from falling into the water.

As she went down on the log, she heard the alligator make a sudden splash in the water. From the corner of her eye, she saw it glide toward her. Faster than she could blink her eyes, it shot out of the water, jaws open, aiming for her dangling foot.

Chapter Eight

Desperately, Morgan yanked up her foot, just as the animal's teeth clanked together, millimeters from her tennis shoe.

She heard a scream and knew it had come from her own throat. But she didn't waste any more energy on terror. Fighting not to plunge into the water, she pulled herself back onto the horizontal surface, teetering as she struggled to keep her body parts out of the jaws of the creature below.

She breathed out a sigh, but she knew she still wasn't safe up here. Not when she'd seen how far the beast could jump out of the water.

The knife was tucked into her belt. She was lucky it hadn't embedded itself in her body during her frantic scramble to stay on the log.

Looking down, she debated what to do. If she left the weapon where it was, both of her hands would be free. But that meant she was defenseless. So she took a moment to free the knife and shouted at the beast to back off as she brandished the weapon. She knew the alligator had a tiny brain, but if it had been threatened before, maybe it had learned caution.

It stayed in the water under her as she carefully crawled along the log toward safety, the knife still clutched in one fist.

Once she reached solid ground, she kept going, putting a dozen yards between herself and the bayou edge before she leaned against a tree trunk, panting, thinking about her narrow escape.

The log had been slippery, as if someone had greased it, hoping she'd fall in and give the alligators a nice meal.

And she would have obliged, if she hadn't thought to take the stick. As she brushed mud off her jeans, she looked back toward the island. She wanted to know what was over there, but not until she figured out a safe way to get across.

So had someone set a trap for her, specifically? Or maybe it wasn't specifically for her. Maybe it was for anyone who came poking around the bayou country at Belle Vista. Who was hiding something out there? Andre? Janet?

Still feeling shaky, she started back toward the house. When she reached the edge of the trees, she remembered another mistake she'd made. She'd forgotten all about the evidence bag with the cigarette butts that she'd dropped on the ground when Sheriff Jarvis had visited the day before.

She walked to the spot where she and Andre had been standing. But the plastic bag was missing.

Muttering under her breath, she traveled several yards farther, searching the site. But the damn bag was definitely gone.

Well, she'd add that to her list of questions for Andre when he finally came home. Grimly she turned back to the house, walking fast, breathing out a small sigh when she reached the lawn.

The day stretched ahead of her. She was trapped at this damn estate. Andre was right; the bayou was dangerous. So was hiking into town—if she was in the mood for that.

Going back to her room, she pulled off her muddy clothing, left them in the hamper and washed the mud off her shoes in the tub before cleaning up the mess and showering.

While she was making herself presentable again, she thought about how she could proceed with her investigation until her car was drivable. Although she was feeling frustrated enough to search Andre's bedroom, the thought of running into Janet was a powerful deterrent.

But maybe the library was a reasonable alternative, she decided.

Downstairs she studied the shelves. Maybe she'd find a local history with a section on the Sonnier-Gascon feud.

She pulled out several local histories and learned how the French settlers had founded St. Germaine and how they'd almost been wiped out by malaria. Fifty years later, the Gascon family had come from France and bought up hundreds of acres in the bayou.

Then she took down a volume of old maps and found something unexpected. Folded inside the front cover was a set of new maps. Well, not regular maps. They seemed to be a geologic survey, as far as she could tell. Maybe she'd found something significant right under her nose.

When she heard footsteps in the hall, she quickly

closed the book and pushed it back onto the shelf, just as Janet stepped into the doorway. "What are you doing?" she asked, her voice sharp, confirming Morgan's suspicion that the woman was keeping a watchful eye on her.

Morgan turned slowly to find the housekeeper standing with a vacuum cleaner in her hand.

"I was going through some of the books."

"Why?"

She fought to keep her voice even and her posture relaxed. "Basically because I was hired to do a job, but I can't get into town until the garage returns my car. I don't feel safe going far from the house, and I can't ask Andre any questions because he's decided to disappear."

Janet made an obvious effort to relax her features. "I'm sorry if you find this situation difficult, child."

Morgan wanted to say she was a fully functioning adult. Instead she murmured, "I'd be justified in going back home and reporting that the client isn't being cooperative."

Alarm clouded Janet's face, and the strength of the woman's reaction startled Morgan.

"Please don't leave."

Morgan folded her arms across her chest. "Give me a reason why I should stay here."

"Because he needs you," she said, sounding like she was struggling to keep her voice steady.

"Then why did he run?"

"He's not running."

"What is he really doing? What can't he get in St. Germaine?"

Janet set down the vacuum cleaner on the hall floor,

looking resigned. "Blame it on me. I told him I couldn't have a visitor here and not be able to bake. The oven thermostat is way out of whack, and I'm afraid I'll burn the house down if I use it. I need a new one, and the only place to get it is an electrical supply company in New Orleans."

"Couldn't you order it?"

"That would take weeks. You're here now."

Morgan nodded, sorry that she'd made an issue of Andre's absence.

"He should be back this afternoon. Then you can tear into him all you like."

Morgan nodded. Before she could ask if she was going to get honest answers, Janet picked up the vacuum and marched down the hall. After waiting for several moments to make sure the woman didn't pop back into the doorway, Morgan opened the book again. Feeling guilty, she took out the maps, then slipped them under her T-shirt.

In her room, she stuffed the papers inside the false bottom of her suitcase, then used the toilet so Janet would hear it flushing.

Back downstairs again, she began looking through more books, but she found no more hidden treasure. After finishing with the history section, she moved to another shelf of old volumes.

The first one she picked up turned out to be *The Erotic Art of Japan,* published in the first decade of the twentieth century. Despite the copyright date, many of the stylized illustrations were quite explicit. They showed Japanese couples engaged in sexual acts of various kinds, some of which looked like they might require the skills of a contortionist. Next to it was a book called *A Day in the Country, An Artistic Study.* The title might be innocuous, but inside were what looked like early twentieth-century photos of men and women picnicking and enjoying other pleasures in a bucolic setting—most of them naked or scantily dressed.

The images were very erotic. Like the naked woman holding out a bowl of apples to a naked man, with her rosy breasts resting on the top of the fruit.

She studied the picture, responding to it on a sensual level, thinking about what made it a turn-on. It wasn't the nudity. The man and woman were looking at each other as if they were going to be each other's next meal.

She was so absorbed in the picture that the sound of someone stepping up behind her made her jump.

"Interesting pictures," a deep voice said behind her.

It was Andre. She knew that even before he spoke because she caught the familiar scent of his body.

"You didn't tell me you collected antique porn," she managed to say, still with her back to him.

"I don't. This is my father's private stash of sexually explicit material. All of it 'collector's items.' I have records of his sending away to dealers around the country."

"Charming."

"Actually, these are some of the volumes that I was thinking about selling. I imagine they would be quite valuable to certain book enthusiasts."

"Yes," she said. He moved closer to her, his front coming into contact with her back as he lifted the book from her hands and set it on the table. Reaching around her, he flipped the pages, then stopped when he came to a photograph of a naked woman sitting in a swing suspended from the branch of a tree, her head thrown back and her face a study in pleasure.

"This is one of my favorites," he said, his voice low and thick.

Morgan focused on the picture. The ropes of the swing were artfully twined with flowering vines. But it wasn't the foliage that drew Morgan's attention. A naked man was holding the ropes. He wasn't behind his partner. Instead he was in front of her, standing with his hips between her spread legs, and either they were having intercourse in that interesting position, or the photographer had faked the scene.

Morgan felt prickles of heat on her skin. "What do you like about it?" she asked.

"The dynamics. It's a still photograph, but it has a strong sense of movement, don't you think?"

As he spoke, he stroked his hands up and down her arms, and she found that the sensations he was creating made it difficult to focus on a coherent answer. "Yes," she managed to say.

"And then there's the sexuality. If you're knowledgeable about lovemaking, you're pretty sure they're locked together. But for someone more naive, it could just be a guy ready to lift a woman off a swing."

"Except that they're both naked," she murmured.

He laughed. "Maybe it's a nudist colony."

"Right." Her voice quavered as he slid his lips along her cheek to her ear, his teeth and tongue playing with the delicate curl.

The sensation was exquisite. Without thinking, she threw her head back like the woman in the picture. He took advantage of the pose to slide his mouth to the side of her neck.

She wanted to turn, but he held her where she was, her body arched, her pulse pounding.

"Did you see the picture of the woman with the bowl of apples?" he asked.

"Yes."

"Another good one." He brought his hands inward, cupping and lifting her breasts. Looking down, she saw the nipples standing out through her shirt. She knew he saw that, too, because he stroked his fingers back and forth over those aching tips.

She made a small, needy sound, asking for more. And he took his cue from her, slipping his hands under her top and touching her through the silky fabric of her bra while he brought his mouth back to the side of her face, her ear.

"Let me turn around," she whispered.

"Don't you like this?"

"You know I do," she said, then tried to change the subject. "What are you hiding from me?"

"Not this," he answered, pressing his erection against her bottom.

When she leaned back against him, she was rewarded by his gasp of pleasure.

He loosened his hold, and she was about to turn when a throat-clearing sound behind them made them both jump.

"I…I surely beg your—your pardon," Janet stammered.

"What do you want?" Andre growled, his tone sharp as his hands dropped to his sides. Morgan was glad he was standing behind her, both of them with their backs to the door.

Janet spoke again. "I came to tell you two men have brought the car back. They want you to pay them so they can clear out as soon as possible."

"I'll be right there," Andre muttered.

"No. I'll do it," Morgan said, closing the book. Mercifully, Janet withdrew.

Morgan took a couple of deep breaths. She had told herself she was not going to get physically involved with Andre again. But all he'd had to do was sneak up behind her and start kissing her ear, and she'd been back in the same trap she'd been helpless to avoid before.

As she walked toward the front of the house, she straightened her shirt. Andre followed her. Because she was angry with herself—and with him—she snapped, "Why did you destroy evidence outside last night?"

"Give me a clue. Evidence of what?"

She stopped and gave him a direct look. "I saw that jaguar in the garden. When I went out to find his tracks, they were gone from the spot where he'd been standing. You raked the area. I had to walk in a big circle to pick up his trail again."

Andre's features registered astonishment. "I didn't rake anything."

She stared at his face, trying to judge whether he was telling the truth or lying through his teeth. He looked genuinely shocked.

"If not you, then who?"

"I don't know," he answered, and this time she wasn't so sure he was telling the truth.

"Do you have a rake besides the one that's locked in your shed?"

"No. But somebody could have brought one," he added.

"Who?"

He only shrugged.

"Did you take away those cigarette butts I found?"

"No!"

Again she studied his face. If he was lying, he was good at it.

"Let me get my purse," she said, then detoured up the steps and into her room.

As she came back down the stairs, she saw that Andre was waiting for her inside.

Through the side light she could see her rental car and another car pulled to the side of the circular drive. Two men were looking nervously around and also up at the sky, which had darkened considerably since that morning. Another man was sitting in the extra car. It was Bob Mansard, who stared balefully at the house.

Morgan glanced at her watch. It was late in the afternoon but the clouds were obviously making it look closer to sunset.

The men turned toward the door when they heard it open. All of them eyed her and Andre. Mansard stayed in the car, and she wondered again if he'd been one of the men who'd followed her from town the day she'd arrived.

One of the standing men could have been his more slender companion, although she couldn't be sure, because of the baseball caps they'd been wearing.

All the men were bareheaded now. The ones in the driveway looked to be in their mid-twenties, with dark hair growing a bit shaggy. One wore overalls; the other was dressed in jeans and a T-shirt.

The guy in overalls shifted his weight from one foot to the other. "We need to be getting on back," he said, his voice coming out gruff and nervous.

"Okay," Morgan said. "How much is the bill?"

He pulled a crumpled sheet of paper out of his overall pocket and handed it to her.

Smoothing out the wrinkles, she read the amount. It was less than she expected.

"I'd like to check the brakes, if you don't mind," she said.

"We have to be getting back." Nervously he glanced at the sky again.

"This will only take a few minutes."

Probably if it had been between her and this man, he would have insisted on leaving right away. Mansard looked as if he, too, was going to add his weight to the discussion. But when Andre took a step closer, the man in overalls stood back and pressed his lips together.

She fished her keys out of her purse, then strode to her car and climbed behind the wheel. After starting the engine, she drove around the circle in front of the house, stopping every so often to make sure the car wasn't acting the way it had on the road. But she couldn't get up much speed so she started down the access road.

Behind her, she heard loud shouts of protest. When she looked back, the man in overalls was running after her, for all the good that was going to do him. Quickly she accelerated to thirty, then slammed on the brakes. They responded well enough, so she made a U-turn and came back to the house.

The men, especially Mansard, were shooting daggers at her as she climbed out, and she almost felt sorry for them. If they were in a hurry to get back, she wasn't helping. But she was enjoying a bit of payback. Not her usual behavior, but today she thought she was justified.

She wrote a check to the gas station, handed it over and added a twenty-dollar bill.

"Thank you for delivering the car," she said sweetly.

"Thank *you*," he responded. Then he added, "We'd best be going."

When they had left, she turned to Andre. "Are they afraid that it's going to rain and there will be another flash flood?"

"Maybe. But I think they're more worried about the cat. The dark sky might make them think it's late enough for the local monster to jump out of the bushes."

"Is it?"

"No," he said sharply, then, "I'll check your car to make sure the work is satisfactory."

"Thank you. Why was Mansard along? As a body-guard?"

"He likes excuses to come out here and stare at me…when he thinks the odds are favorable."

"Nice."

Andre gave a shrug, looking uncomfortable.

Now that they were alone, she felt uncomfortable, too, as she remembered what they had been doing in the library when Janet had interrupted them. What was his reaction now? Was he sorry that he'd started something? Or was he thinking about how quickly she'd responded? She should remind him that they were going to keep their relationship on a professional level. But she could hardly blame the whole incident on him. He'd found her looking at dirty pictures, after all. Then he'd come up behind her—close behind—and she'd welcomed his touch.

She was angry with herself for reacting to him. Angry at him for putting her in that position. And angry that the easy relationship they'd established while she was still in Baltimore had suddenly changed when she'd gotten down here.

She had planned to bombard him with questions, but now she needed to put some distance between them. So she went up to her room until dinner—where she gave herself a silent lecture on client-investigator relations.

By the time she came down, she'd determined to get things back on the right track. To her disappointment, only two places were set at the table. Since Morgan wasn't in the mood to spend the meal trying to make conversation with Janet, she said she was worn-out and took a tray up to her room.

After checking in with Light Street, she turned in early and slept through the night again.

THE NEXT DAY she woke up feeling refreshed—and eager to confront Andre with some of the questions he should already have answered—like was he keeping pet alligators out by the fallen log.

Her plans were put on hold again when he failed to appear once more. Now she knew he was avoiding her. Because he was embarrassed about yesterday? Or because he didn't want to discuss the case he'd hired her to investigate?

"He's gone off to cut up some trees that were uprooted in the storm," Janet explained.

"Oh, right," Morgan answered, unable to keep the sarcasm out of her voice. "Did he fix the oven first?"

"Yes." The housekeeper held out a basket of cinnamon buns. "I was able to make these for you."

Morgan instantly regretted taking out her bad mood on Janet. She had to keep remembering that the housekeeper wasn't controlling the situation. Andre was the one making the decisions.

She took one of the buns, and the first bite told her that the lack of an oven had truly deprived her of a rare experience. "These are wonderful," she said.

Janet beamed. "I wanted to make them for you."

The buns put Morgan in a better mood.

After licking icing off her fingers, she got up and opened the back door, listening to the sound of a chain saw somewhere in the distance. So Janet hadn't been lying. Andre had gone out into the bayou to saw up logs.

She thought about marching out into the wilderness area, following the sound. Then she decided that wouldn't do her much good. He had an excellent way to keep from engaging in conversation. All he had to do was continue sawing.

Morgan went back upstairs and got a carry bag. Then she retrieved the maps she'd hidden in the special compartment of her suitcase. As far as she could tell, nobody had found it. But there was no way to be sure.

With the maps in her bag, she went down to her car and started toward St. Germaine, driving slowly, testing the brakes every half mile, making sure they were working. When they proved reliable, she sped up a bit, then slowed when she came to the place where the water had washed across the road and almost swept her away. The site of the flood was very clear, and she pulled to a stop. As she looked at the uprooted trees, logjams of man-made and natural debris and mud sweeping across the road, a clogged feeling rose in her throat.

She tried to move her foot, tried to press down on the gas pedal. But her muscles wouldn't obey. It was like an invisible force held her in place, making it impossible for her to keep driving.

In her mind she heard the deadly roar of onrushing water. It was coming for her again.

No. The sun was shining. She was in no danger. Not today.

Still, some part of her waited for the water to come and sweep her away. And this time Andre couldn't save her.

No, that was wrong. He could save her. He *had* saved her. He had appeared out of nowhere and dragged her to shore.

Her hands tightened on the wheel as she fought the sensation of being pulled under and carried away. That hadn't happened. Andre had plunged into the current and hauled her to safety.

Chapter Nine

Morgan clung to the steering wheel, fighting terror that threatened to swallow her whole. She wanted to jump out of the car and run screaming into the bayou. Until she remembered the snakes and the alligators and maybe the jaguar.

"Stop it!" she ordered herself. "Stop it. You're safe and dry in the car. You're not in danger here."

Yet she knew some force outside herself was affecting her perception of the world.

"You're safe and dry," she repeated over and over, even as she fought the sensation of water clawing at her, dragging her under. She wasn't even sure what she was doing, but somehow she got control of herself.

The terror ebbed, the way the water had ebbed in the real flood, leaving her limp and shaken. She sat behind the wheel, dragging in air and forcing herself to breathe out slowly.

When she felt in control, she glanced around at the wilderness landscape. Something lying on the shoulder caught her eye, something dark and evil looking.

Gris-gris.

She wanted to stay inside the car where the evil

couldn't touch her. Then she reminded herself she wasn't going to pieces over a voodoo charm.

Grimly she firmed her jaw and climbed out, feeling muggy heat envelope her as she stood on shaky legs, one hand on the door. When she felt she could stay erect on her own, she tottered across the road, her eyes fixed on the black charm—which turned out to be a small lump of tar, studded with foreign objects, like the one she and Andre had found outside the library window.

Straw and moss and a strip of paper were stuck to it. But what caught her eye was a scrap of limp and soggy leather. And she gasped as she recognized what it was— part of a sandal she had lost in the flood.

Without thinking about what she was doing, she kicked out her foot, connected with the thing and booted it into the water, where it floated on the surface for several seconds, then sank with a gurgling sound.

The moment it disappeared from view, she knew she had let emotion sweep away reason. The gris-gris was evidence—and she had just chucked it into the water.

She was a disciplined, trained operative, yet she'd acted in panic. A film of sweat dampened her body as she stared for a long moment at the place where the evil charm had disappeared below the surface of the water. No way could she retrieve it now.

Her knit top was clinging wetly to her upper body as she scrambled back into the vehicle and slammed the door. Jamming her foot on the gas pedal, she made the car lurch as she started toward town again.

Her heart had just settled down to a calmer rhythm when she spotted the voodoo priestess's house. Most likely the woman had left the charm on the road. What if Morgan stopped and demanded to know why?

And what if someone else had done it to incriminate the priestess?

She wanted to slow down and look at the house. She wanted to speed up and flee from danger.

Somehow she kept the car moving at a steady pace as she passed the dwelling. By the time she reached Main Street, she had convinced herself she was feeling almost normal.

There were few people in town, and when she cut her engine in front of a convenience store that offered fax service, hers was the only car.

As she walked toward the door, she was thinking she would have preferred to fax the material in private. But her laptop couldn't handle hard copy. And if she used the machine in Andre's office, he'd have a record of the transaction.

In the parking lot, she used her cell phone to call the shop in the lobby at 43 Light Street.

Her friend Sabrina Cassidy answered.

"Hi. It's Morgan," she said, feeling a wave of home-sickness sweep over her. After Trevor had died, she'd wondered how she was going to survive. The support of her Light Street friends had probably saved her life. Now she was far away from their help.

"Morgan! You're on assignment in Louisiana, right?"

"I guess the news made it to the jungle telegraph," she joked.

"So, did you just want to talk to a friendly voice, or are you making a clandestine phone call?" Sabrina asked.

"Actually, it's about a clandestine fax. Can I send a couple of sheets to you so the office number doesn't appear on the transmission?"

"Of course."

"They'll be arriving soon. If you could take them upstairs and give them to Sam Lassiter, or whoever is on
duty, I'd appreciate it."

"No problem."

"And if anybody asks you, say they're inquiries
about some books my employer might want to sell."

"Will do."

After thanking her friend, Morgan went into the
store. As she approached the counter, the clerk did a
double take.

"Something wrong?" she asked, trying not to sound
confrontational.

"You're the librarian, right?" he asked.

She sighed. Apparently everybody in town knew
who she was. "Yes. Can I use your fax machine?"

"How many pages?"

"Two."

"The machine will tell you the charges."

"Thanks."

He looked speculatively at her book bag. "Need
some help?"

"I think I can manage," she answered, hoping the response didn't come out sounding too sharp. "Where's
the fax?"

He pointed to a service area near the rest rooms. Before he could insist on helping, she was rescued as a
woman came in and asked for a cup of coffee.

While the clerk was busy, Morgan scanned the in-
structions.

The second map was halfway through the machine
when the door opened and another customer walked in.
This time she recognized the ruddy complexion and

blond hair of Dwight Rivers, the president of the chamber of commerce. When he spotted her, he strode in her direction. Morgan gave the map a tug, hoping she hadn't screwed up the transmission, then stuffed the paper into the carry bag.

Rivers eyed her. "You could have come to me if you needed to send a fax."

"Oh, thank you. I didn't know that."

"I guess you weren't just vacationing in town," he observed with an edge in his voice.

She gave him an apologetic smile. "You probably heard about my run-in at the gas station. I didn't want to get into another discussion about Andre Gascon."

"Right. I understand. But I'm not like those guys."

She answered with a small nod, turning her shoulder away from him.

Ignoring her body language, he asked, "Doesn't he have a fax machine?"

"It's broken."

He shoved his hands into his pockets. "Aside from that, how are things going out at the estate?"

"Fine."

"Good you got your car back."

"Yes." She kept her eyes on his and asked, "So what brings you out in the heat of the day?"

He waited a beat before answering, "We're out of tea bags at the office."

"Mmm-hmm." She knew how small towns worked. Probably somebody had called him and said that the librarian was in town and that she'd gone to the convenience store.

He took a step closer. "You know, I always thought Gascon got a raw deal from the town. I mean their blaming him for stuff going on in the bayou just because it's near his house."

"Why do you think it happened?"

"Partly because he keeps to himself so much. People get suspicious of a guy who isn't friendly, who doesn't fit in."

Morgan nodded, thinking that Rivers was twisting the facts. Andre had come into St. Germaine a lot more often before other people had started looking at him with suspicion. But she didn't bother to argue the point.

"You take care," Rivers said as he turned and walked down one of the aisles.

With the fax sent, Morgan drove to the gun store. After a few moments' hesitation, she took the carry bag with her and walked toward the front door of the shop. The sign in the window said Jacques Malvaux, Proprietor. The man himself—at least she assumed it was him—was leaning against the counter cleaning a twenty-two revolver.

"I'm guessing that's unloaded," she said.

"What do you think I am, soft in the head?" he asked.

"Of course not. I just like to make sure."

"I didn't know librarians had a lot of call for guns," he drawled, looking her up and down.

"My father was a gun collector," she answered. "He wanted me to know how to handle a weapon, how to defend myself."

"Always a useful skill. So what can I do for you?" Malvaux asked, leaning back comfortably. When his gaze flicked to the window, she turned, but she saw nothing beyond the shop but the street.

"I'm out in the country where anything could happen. I'd like a Glock model twenty-three, if you have one," she answered.

"So you're a little lady who wants the stopping power of a forty-caliber weapon, with reduced size for easy concealment."

"Yes," she answered, thinking that the gun part was right. The "little lady" part made her stomach curdle.

"Lucky for you there are no concealed-weapons laws in this state."

"Right. Lucky for me."

"If you're recoil-sensitive, you might want to try one of the Glock C models."

"I think I can handle the twenty-three," she informed him primly.

"Okeydoke." He unlocked the case in front of him, reached inside and brought out an automatic that was much like the one she'd lost. When he set it on the counter, she picked it up and checked out the mechanism, then turned and sighted down the barrel.

"This will do."

"You make up your mind fast."

"Mmm-hmm."

"I have to enter your application into the national database and make sure you don't have a criminal record."

"All right."

He made a photocopy of her driver's license, then handed it back before beginning to type slowly into a computer.

Finally he turned back to her. "All set."

She gestured toward the gun. "Three refillable magazines come with it, right?"

"Correct. Holding ten rounds each."

She nodded. "And I'd like a box of bullets."

Malvaux chuckled. "You sure you don't want silver bullets?"

"Why?" she demanded.

"For that supernatural jaguar out in the bayou near Belle Vista."

The way he said it sent a shiver slithering down her spine.

She kept her voice even as she said, "You're saying the jaguar is supernatural?"

"I guess you'll find out."

"Why don't you tell me more about the town legends?"

"Legends…well, I don't know about that." His face had a closed expression as he put her purchases into a plastic bag, and she suspected he'd decided he was sorry he'd brought up the subject.

As she exited the store, she felt his eyes boring into her back.

When she reached her car, she stopped short and muttered a very unlibrarianlike curse.

While she'd been inside, someone had slashed her left rear tire with a knife—and she'd be willing to bet, from the way that Jacques Malvaux had glanced at the window, that he'd seen the perp.

She'd turned in response, but whoever was out there had already ducked down so that the car hid him. Then he could have crawled away like a yellow-bellied gator.

She grimaced. Was the tire slashing malicious fallout from the campaign against Andre? Or was someone interested in seeing how the little lady librarian handled a flat tire?

Opening the trunk, she checked the tool kit and was relieved to find a jack, which she dragged out and set under the bumper.

It took her under half an hour to get the ruined tire

off and the new one onto the wheel. After that, she wanted to drive straight back to Belle Vista, but because that would leave her without a spare, she drove to the gas station, sure that everyone in town was peering out from behind their curtains, watching her. Bob Mansard gave her a satisfied look as she stopped in the service area, making her wonder if he was the one who had slashed the tire.

"Problems?" Bubba asked helpfully, like he already knew what had happened.

"A flat. I'm pretty sure it's beyond repair, so I'm hoping you have a replacement." She gave him the number, then waited while he checked his stock.

When he produced a substitute, she put it into the trunk herself, figuring she wasn't going to give him another crack at screwing up the vehicle.

As she headed out of town, she looked in the rearview mirror to make sure no one was behind her. Then she pulled onto the shoulder, retrieved the Glock from the shopping bag and loaded it. One thing she liked about the weapon was the safety system. The only way it could fire was if your finger was on the trigger, which made her feel okay about slipping a loaded gun into her purse.

When she reached the house, neither Janet nor Andre was around. But there was a new pile of cut and split wood near the back door.

Thinking that luck was with her for once, Morgan walked quietly inside and into the library. The book where the maps had been concealed was in the same place. After a glance over her shoulder, she put the sheets back where she'd found them, then breathed out a little sigh before going up to her room to leave the carry bag. Since the incident with the alligator and the log, she'd vowed that she wasn't going to go tramping around the estate armed with just a kitchen knife. So she kept her purse strap slung over her shoulder as she hurried downstairs and outside again.

The saw was buzzing again, but she set off across the lawn, heading toward the sound, thinking Andre had cut enough wood for one day.

She hadn't been to this part of the grounds before. At the edge of the lawn she came to a slate path that led under the trees, and she followed it to a three-foot-tall wrought-iron fence. Beyond it were several white horizontal objects. As she drew closer, they resolved themselves into aboveground crypts.

Apparently she'd stumbled across the family graveyard. To her eyes, the coffin-shaped burial chambers looked strange, but she remembered that down here they were the norm.

As she walked slowly forward, it registered somewhere in her consciousness that the sound of the saw had stopped, leaving her in a bubble of silence.

The cemetery plot was not as well tended as the rest of the grounds. Weeds poked up through the dark earth, a rose climbed along one side of the fence and leaves were scattered across the graying tops of the crypts.

A small inner voice warned her to walk away from this place. Instead Morgan pushed at the gate. The hinges squeaked, grating on her nerve endings. The moment she entered the enclosure, the temperature felt as if it dropped ten degrees, and she looked down at the fingers of fog that began rising from the ground.

Fog. Only here?

She wanted to get out of this place. But somehow the

mist twisted around her ankles and held her, the way something had held her at the scene of the flood, she thought with a shudder.

Run. Get away, a voice in her head warned. Instead she kept moving forward.

She could hear a noise in the background now. Not the saw. Was it more like the beating of a drum? Wrapping her hands over her arms, she rubbed her chilled skin. It felt as though she had stepped into a supernatural place. Or some supernatural force had taken over the graveyard. Taken over *her.*

Shadows flickered around her, creating the illusion that the little cemetery was haunted by the ghosts from the past. And something from the present, too—a force that pressed against her, making it hard to breathe.

She looked up, seeing the tree branches overhead swaying in the wind, shifting the patterns of light and dark around her, blurring her vision.

Someone called her name, a ghostly sound carried away by the wind.

She straightened her shoulders, struggling to put the idea of specters out of her head as she moved reluctantly toward the nearest crypt. Brushing away the leaves, she saw that the name was almost completely worn away, but as she squinted at the carved letters, she saw that a Margot Gascon was buried here.

Who was the woman? Morgan didn't know. But she understood that it was important to look at the other names. One name in particular. She must find it.

She was moving frantically now, hurrying through the cemetery. A grave at the back drew her. That was the one. Yes. She knew it, even though she couldn't see the name yet.

Leaning over the flat top of the crypt, she brushed frantically at the leaves, then tried to read the worn letters. At first she couldn't make any sense of the words. With a shaking hand, she traced the carving. The stone felt like ice against her fingertips. When the name came into focus, she gasped.

It said Andre Gascon.

Instinctively she leaped back, then bumped into something that hadn't been there before.

Not something. Someone.

Two separate and distinct thoughts vied for prominence in her frantically scrambling mind. The men from town had followed her to this isolated location and were going to finish what they'd started on the road. Or one of the ghosts she'd sensed in this place of death had sneaked up behind her.

If the men were after her, her next act might have been rational. Fumbling in her purse, she pulled out the gun she'd just bought and slipped her finger through the trigger guard as she whirled around, prepared to shoot the enemy.

Her heart leaped into her throat when she found herself facing Andre.

He was wearing a T-shirt, jeans and muddy work boots. His face and shirt were streaked with perspiration, and he was staring at her with an expression that mirrored her own shock.

"Put down the gun," he said in a steady voice.

"You're dead," she gasped, backing away from him, bumping into another crypt. Somewhere in her brain, she knew she wasn't thinking rationally. Andre was standing in front of her—alive and well. He had been out in the bayou working and he had followed her into the cemetery.

Still she kept seeing the white burial chamber imposed on his image, and she kept the gun pointed at him, the weight of the weapon reassuring.

"No. I'm very much alive."

"But…your name." Without lowering the weapon, she gestured toward the crypt.

"That's my grandfather."

"Your grandfather," she repeated. Suddenly she felt dizzy. Closing her eyes, she pressed her free hand to her temple. "Andre, what just happened to me?" she whispered.

He answered with his own question. "Where did you get that gun?"

"In town," she said, lowering the weapon, feeling now like it was weighing down her hand.

"Put it away before somebody gets hurt."

"Right." As she eased her finger away from the trigger and carefully put the weapon back in her purse, realization slammed into her.

"I could have shot you," she wheezed.

"You didn't."

"What's happening to me?" she asked again, fighting the pain in her head.

"I don't know."

Suddenly it was important to explain why she had been so startled. "There are no dates on the gravestone," she whispered.

He kept his voice even. "They're at the foot of each marker." He moved past her, brushed away leaves and pointed.

She made out the dates. Andre's grandfather had been born in the late 1800s, died in the 1970s.

"You knew him?" she asked.

"When I was a boy. He was pretty old when I was born," Andre said, then cleared his throat. "Let's get out of here."

"Yes." She wanted to get as far away as she could from this place. When he took her hand and led her to the gate, she followed willingly. But something glistening on the ground made her stop short, a strangled sound bubbling in her throat.

Chapter Ten

Andre shoved Morgan protectively behind him. "What is it?" he asked urgently.

She pointed to the gris-gris. "Another one. It's another one."

Still shielding her, he knelt and pushed the weeds aside, then swore. Prepared with another handkerchief, he scooped the gris-gris up and closed his fist around it.

"It did that to me," she whispered.

"Did what?"

"Messed with my mind. Made me reach for my gun and almost shoot you."

"Unfortunately, you may be right," he said as he led her outside the fence and closed the gate.

She gulped. "I saw another one today."

He whirled toward her. "Another charm? Where?"

"On the road into town. Near where you rescued me from the flood."

"And what happened?" he demanded.

"I felt like the water was sweeping me away, even though I was safe in the car."

His face turned fierce. *"Merde!"*

"Is it the priestess?"

"Who else has that power?"

She shook her head. She hadn't believed in supernatural power at all. Now it looked as if she had no choice.

"You should go back to the house," he said.

She knew he wanted to protect her. She was also pretty sure he was looking for an excuse to withdraw behind the wall he'd built around himself since she'd arrived.

"This time, stay and talk to me," she whispered. "Why are you so different from the man I thought I knew?"

His gaze burned into her. "What do you mean—the man you thought you knew?"

She forced herself to speak frankly. "I mean, when we sent e-mail messages back and forth, you...you seemed friendly and open. We exchanged a lot of information. Not just about the case. Personal stuff. Then, as soon as I got here, you started being...evasive."

He clenched and unclenched his fists. "The first thing that happened when you got here was men from town threatening you in the bayou. I realized I'd put you in danger by asking you to come to Belle Vista."

"But not giving me information doesn't help!"

"I'm trying to figure out what to do!"

"Well, you can't do it on your own. You hired me to do a job. Let me do it." She struggled to get control of her own emotions. Fumbling her way back to a less threatening topic, she said, "Tell me about the graveyard."

His face contorted. "My ancestors are buried here. I don't visit them often, so I tend to neglect the place."

"You could hire someone."

"There aren't many people around here who would work for me."

The flat way he said it tore at her. But she needed more than words. Reaching out, she wrapped him in her arms.

"You should stay away from me," he whispered.

"Why?"

"Like I said, I'm putting you in danger."

"From whom?"

"From the voodoo priestess. And from whoever is trying to drive me away from Belle Vista."

"When you hired me, you didn't say anyone was trying to drive you away."

"Because it's hard to talk about something that disturbing."

"So you thought you'd get me down here, then work it into the conversation."

He laughed. "Something like that."

"Well, I'm prepared to hear anything you have to say. I'm not some little librarian from Baltimore. I'm a trained undercover agent."

"Right. Tough as forged steel," he murmured, and she caught a hint of the very appealing man she remembered from their correspondence.

Was that why she'd come down to Louisiana? Because she'd enjoyed his company long-distance? And was that part of the instant physical attraction she'd felt for him?

She had fought that attraction. Now she heard herself say, "Maybe neither one of us is as tough as we think."

When he didn't answer, she said, "I'm here. You don't have to go it alone."

His arms slipped around her shoulders. When he'd held her before, his touch had turned passionate. Now he was deliberately keeping them both at a less-heated level.

"Tell me about the curse," she whispered.

She half expected him to pull away. Instead he dragged in a breath, then let it out. "I told you I didn't go away to school because I had to take care of my father. That was true, but it wasn't the only reason. I can't leave this place. So whoever is trying to drive me away is doomed to failure." He laughed, and this time the sound wasn't pleasant. "The joke's on them."

"What do you mean you can't leave?"

His teeth clamped together, then he seemed to make a deliberate effort to relax. "The priestess comes out here to reinforce an old grudge. Her ancestor cursed my family. We have to stay at Belle Vista."

She tipped her head back, staring into his eyes. "You believe that?"

"Yes."

"Why?"

"You said you felt the power—on the road and now in the graveyard."

"Yes," she admitted.

"I feel it, too." He grimaced. "If we put it in medical terms, we could say that what you experienced were acute episodes. What I've got is a low-level, persistent infection that flares up if I stay away from Belle Vista for too long."

"If you stay away overnight?" she guessed.

"Yes."

"And what happens here at night?"

She saw him swallow. "I have to go out into the bayou…and stay there until near dawn."

"But isn't that dangerous?"

"Yes. But I have no choice, so I've learned to live with it."

"Can you break the curse?" she asked in a shaky voice, amazed that she had bought in to the reality of a voodoo curse. But she'd discovered it was the only way to have a coherent discussion about his problems.

"Maybe if I had someone at my side to help." He swallowed. "Someone willing to stay here with me."

She nodded silently, not sure what to say.

His eyes drilled into hers. She wanted to look away, but she held herself steady. Another question burned behind her lips. A question she was afraid to ask. Yet Andre had finally been honest with her. Now she had to face her own fears about the dreams she'd had since she'd put on the robe.

"The woman your grandfather loved and lost—was her name Linette Sonnier?" she whispered.

Morgan watched a host of emotions chasing themselves across Andre's face. "Where did you get that name?" he asked in a hoarse voice.

"Where could I have gotten it?" she asked carefully.

His jaw firmed. "You could have researched my family."

"Well, that's not how the name came to me," she answered.

He opened his mouth, but she hurried on, forcing herself to grapple with one of the other questions that had been gnawing at her since the first afternoon when Andre had rescued her from the flood. "Why was that robe you gave me in a bag of clothing in your car?"

"I told you, it was going to a garage sale at the church."

"You don't get along with the town, so why were you taking anything to a church sale?" she challenged.

"It was either that or burn the clothing, and I was taught from a young age never to throw out anything that someone could use. Just because some people in St. Germaine don't like me is no reason to spite the rest of them."

"Okay." She would give him that much. But it still didn't get to the crux of her question. "You didn't have the robe—" She stopped then began again. "You didn't have the robe in the car so I could put it on?"

Instead of answering, he made a frustrated gesture with his hand. "I asked you about Linette. What does that have to do with the bag of clothing? I didn't even know it was in there until you were sitting there shivering like a drowned muskrat. Why are we going on about the robe?"

Lifting her gaze, she looked back toward the cemetery plot. It was no longer visible through the trees, but she knew it was still lurking in the shadows. "I had a couple of weird experiences today."

"And? This is the damn strangest conversation I ever had," he added in exasperation. "Are you just going to ignore every question I ask you?"

"I'm working up to an answer," she murmured, scuffing her foot against the ground, watching with great interest as she scraped a line in the dirt. "This is hard. What I wanted to say was that I...had another weird experience when I put on the robe." She swallowed.

"A bad experience?"

"No. I...I had a vision of Linette."

His reaction seemed to be as strong as her own. "What?" he gasped out. "What are you talking about?"

"Andre, I'm a pretty down-to-earth person. I don't know how to describe what happened exactly. It was like I had a dream. About her."

"While you were sitting in the car, right after I pulled you out of the water? When you looked like you were asleep?"

"Yes," she answered. Then, because she wanted to be honest, she said, "And later, when I went to bed that first night I was here."

He gave her an appraising look. "A dream. If you're in a dream, you'd be one of the characters. So who were you?"

It was a very perceptive question. She wanted to duck away from his probing gaze, but she wasn't going to be a coward, so she kept her eyes focused on him. "I was Linette."

His indrawn breath raised goose bumps on her skin, but she struggled to stay rational. "What do you know about it?" she demanded.

When he didn't answer, a terrible notion leaped into her mind. "Tell me what's going on, damn you! Were you projecting some sort of dream into my head? Is that it?"

"No! How could I do something like that?" he returned.

"I don't know! If you didn't hypnotize me, then what?"

She saw his hands clench, then unclench. Slowly and distinctly he said, "I don't know what happened to *you,* but I've dreamed about Linette for years."

She stared at him. Then the obvious question tumbled from her lips, the question he'd asked her. "And in those dreams who are *you?*"

For a moment she thought he was going to walk away instead of answering. He dragged shaky fingers through his hair. "I'm Andre. My grandfather. Myself. Hell, I don't know anymore!"

Stunned, she tried to cope with the implications—just as the sounds of shouting and banging made them both look up. Once again someone had interrupted their conversation before she could find out what she needed to know.

Andre took off toward the house. Morgan followed him. When they arrived at the front of the building, they found a man pounding on the door with his big fists. He had obviously come here to make trouble, and Morgan gripped her purse, wondering if she was going to need her gun.

"Show your face, you bastard," the guy shouted. "Show face."

"I take it you're talking to me," Andre said calmly from the driveway.

The man whirled. "Yeah, you."

He came charging down the steps, his hands still balled into fists and his eyes flashing.

Morgan tensed and slipped her hand into her purse.

Glancing at Andre, she saw he was standing with his arms dangling casually at his sides. But the tension in his shoulders told her he was ready to repel an attack.

"What's the problem, Carl?" he asked.

"Where were you when my brother brung that car yesterday?"

"I was here with Ms. Kirkland. What's the problem?" Andre asked again.

"What did you do to my brother?" the man demanded.

"Your brother, Rick Brevard?"

"You damn well know who I mean." His gaze swung to Morgan. "Did you see him yesterday?"

"If he was one of the men who delivered the car, yes," she answered.

Andre took a protective step closer to her. "Could you tell us what this is all about?"

"The last I saw Rick, he was on his way out here, driving your rental car."

"And he left again," she said quickly. "With another man."

"Henri Dauphin. I was damn well expecting them yesterday evening. They're not back."

"I'm sorry. I can't help you," Andre said.

"Where were you all day?" Brevard demanded. "And last night?"

"Last night I was sleeping," Andre said evenly, his gaze flicking to Morgan.

A few minutes ago he'd said he was in the swamp. Had he slept there? He must have. He couldn't stay up twenty-four hours a day.

"Today I was in the bayou to saw some logs and split them for firewood."

"So you say."

"Well, the fresh-cut logs are by the back door," Andre said. "And I can help you look for the men."

"I don't need your help!"

"Then why are you here?"

"To tell you they'd better show up."

"I hope they do," Morgan answered.

"Yeah, you'd *better* hope so," the man growled, his eyes on Andre. For a long moment they stood facing each other, and Morgan was afraid Carl Brevard might do something stupid. Instead he brushed past them, climbed into his car and slammed the door.

As he roared down the drive, Morgan breathed out a little sigh and pulled her hand from her purse.

"What were you going to do—pull a gun on him?" Andre asked.

"How did you know?"

"I saw your hand go into your purse."

"It was an option," she murmured.

"But not a very good one."

She shifted her weight from one foot to the other. "I would have done it if I needed to."

"You don't want to get arrested because of me."

"You think that would have happened?"

"*Chère,* the least little thing that happens around here they call the cops."

She nodded, then changed the subject. "What do you think happened to the men who brought the car yesterday?"

"You saw them drive away." He shrugged his shoulders. "I don't know what happened, but I think I'd better go look for them."

"Let me help."

"No," he said quickly and firmly. "If something happened in the bayou, I want you safe in the house. Is that understood?"

"I could help you," she insisted. "Two sets of eyes are better than one."

"Not necessarily. I told you, I know my way around the backcountry since I'm there every night. I know how to avoid the dangers. If you were with me, I'd only worry about you. And your going off by yourself is out of the question."

"Carl could be waiting to jump you."

Andre nodded tightly. She wanted to insist on going with him, wanted to say she would be worried every moment he was gone, but she kept those words locked inside and clamped a hand on his arm. "You're willing to help him? Even if he hates you?"

His gaze scorched hers. "Especially if he hates me."

A noise from the landing made her glance up, and she saw Janet gazing down at her, looking upset.

"Come in," she said to Morgan in a quiet but insistent voice.

Two against one, Morgan told herself. She still could have protested, but now she and Andre had an audience.

Lowering her voice, she said, "We have to talk about Linette and Andre."

"Yes."

At least he'd conceded that much, although maybe he was just agreeing so she'd stop arguing with him.

"I have to go," he added. "Don't make me worry about you tonight. Promise me you'll stay inside."

"All right," she whispered. Then, before she could change her mind, she climbed the steps. At the top, she turned and stared down at Andre, who was looking up at her. "Stay safe," he growled.

Then, stiffly, he turned and trotted away. She wanted to ask what he was thinking right now, where he would look for the men and how he could possibly locate them in all that wilderness. Instead she watched him disappear into the trees.

Shoulders slumped, Morgan followed Janet into the house.

"He told you he goes into the swamp at night?" the housekeeper asked.

"Yes."

"That's more than he's told anyone else."

"And what do you know about it?" Morgan demanded.

"I won't give away his secrets, child," the woman said before turning away.

Morgan wanted to follow her into the kitchen and demand a better answer, but she knew she'd be wasting her time. Janet was loyal—and stubborn.

Instead she went up to her room and tried to do some online research. But she couldn't find anything on the history of Linette Sonnier and Andre Gascon.

A knock at the door made her glance up sharply.

"Come in," she called out.

Janet opened the door. "Would you like to have dinner?" the housekeeper asked.

After a silent debate, she answered, "Well, I've had a pretty tiring day. Would you mind if I just took a sandwich up here?"

"Since I got the oven back, I made a nice shepherd's pie. You could have some of that."

"That sounds wonderful," Morgan said. "I was just trying not to make any extra work for you."

"The dinner's already made. You can eat on the sunporch," Janet said quickly.

Morgan wasn't sure what the polite thing to do was, but she decided that Janet might not want her company, either, so she followed the housekeeper downstairs, then took a tray of food out to a room at the side of the house where she hadn't been before. It was furnished with wicker chairs and a wrought-iron patio set. Several ficus trees and pots of flowers were set around on the slate floor. Through the big windows she could look out at the last glimmers of light from the sunset.

The view would have been appealing if she'd been able to relax and enjoy it.

Although she had very little appetite, she knew that Janet had gone to the trouble of making dinner, so she finished as much of it as she could—which wasn't very much.

When she took the tray back to the kitchen, she was relieved to find the room empty. After a quick glance over her shoulder, she scraped the food on her plate into the disposal and ran the appliance before putting the plate in the dishwasher.

Up in her room, she stood at the window for a long time, wishing she could see something—even a light in the swamp—but it was pitch-dark. How could Andre function out there?

Bone-deep worry gnawed at her. If he were anywhere else besides the middle of a swamp, she would have gone outside to look for him. But she knew that tramping into the bayou was as dangerous as it was futile.

Again she tried to distract herself. As she did most evenings, she checked her e-mail. At least there was something to take her mind off Andre—a message from Light Street.

Jo O'Malley had looked at the maps Morgan had sent and confirmed they seemed to be a geological survey. Since she wasn't familiar with the notation, she was sending them to an expert. Morgan should expect to hear something in a day or two.

After thanking Jo, Morgan looked at some of the bulletin board digests. The messages simply didn't hold her interest. Finally she gave up, took a shower and pulled on clean panties and a T-shirt. Always prepared to get out of bed quickly, she placed a pair of jeans over the arm of a chair.

She lay in bed for a long time, listening for Andre to come in, and finally drifted off. The sound of chanting startled her awake. It took a moment for her to figure out where she was and what she was hearing.

The damn voodoo priestess was back.

Morgan felt her throat close, felt a wave of dizziness sweep over her. She jumped out of bed, then had to grab the edge of the mattress to keep from falling over. It took several moments before she felt steady enough to walk.

Still, her steps were shaky as she crossed the room, then stood at the window, breathing hard.

She felt as if she were trying to function underwater. After her experiences on the road and in the graveyard, the woman's voice and the sound of the drum seemed to reach her on a deeper level. They pounded at the frayed edges of her sanity.

The words beat in her head. She had to get away. Out of this room. Out of the house. Out of Louisiana. If she didn't leave, she would die. She knew that at a gut-wrenching, fear-ridden level.

Panic clawed at her chest, at her throat.

"You will not fall apart. It's just a woman out there trying to scare you," she ordered herself. "Stop it this minute."

Her fingers dug into her palms as she fought to catch her breath. Panting, she focused on the pain as she struggled to ground herself.

The fingernails digging into her flesh helped bring her mind back to reality. She had been caught in the grip of a panic attack, that was all. The woman was trying to put her under a spell, only now she had a better idea how to fight against it.

"You shouldn't have left those charms. I'm on to you now," she muttered. "I'm not going to let you scare me."

Taking several seconds to catch her breath, she looked out into the darkness, searching under the trees. At first her eyes could see little in the blackness. When she had adjusted to the low light, she zeroed in on the spot where she'd seen the priestess the first night at the estate.

This time she saw nothing. Blinking, she stared harder. But she wasn't mistaken. The woman wasn't there, and she felt a spurt of disappointment.

She had been so sure she would find the priestess.... Still, the chanting hadn't stopped.

Again fear leaped up, blocked her windpipe.

Not fear for herself. For Andre. He was outside in the dark. He had told her that the priestess hated him, that her curse had some kind of power over him. Maybe this time the chant was meant for Andre. And maybe a voodoo charm had already done something to the men who were missing.

Whirling away from the window, Morgan grabbed her jeans and quickly pulled them on. Scuffing her feet into shoes, she looked toward her purse. Her gun was in there and she wanted the comfort of its weight in her hand, but after the episode in the graveyard, she knew that taking it could be dangerous. The wrong person could get shot, especially in the dark.

Throwing open her door, she started for the stairs. She was halfway down the hall when someone grabbed her from behind.

Chapter Eleven

Morgan went into a martial arts crouch, ready to fight off whoever had grabbed her.

It was Janet, and the woman's eyes widened as she stared at Morgan's defensive stance.

"Don't hurt me, child," she said, her voice quavering. "I didn't mean anything bad."

"Why did you grab me?"

"You were going out. Like that woman wanted you to do."

"The priestess?"

"Yes."

"I'm still going out," Morgan said.

"You can't."

"Andre's out there. She may be after him."

"He can take care of himself," Janet snapped.

"But…"

"Andre can take care of himself," Janet repeated. "It's important for you to stay inside where you're safe."

"Why?"

The housekeeper gave her a long look. "Because he needs you."

"For what?"

Janet continued to stare at her. "You have to figure that out for yourself."

The woman's words were spoken in a low voice. But they hit Morgan with a staggering force. The chanting from outside wrapped itself around her. "What are you doing to me? All of you?" she gasped.

"You have to be strong," Janet said softly.

"I thought I was strong. Now…"

"Go back to your room. Get some rest. You have a lot to face in the morning."

"How do you know?"

Janet hesitated, then said, "I have the sight."

"What does that mean?"

"It's in my blood. Not like my cousin's, but I know things."

"What things?"

"That you should be in bed now."

Maybe it was the firm way Janet said it, but Morgan turned around and went back to her room.

With fingers that felt thick and clumsy, she pulled off her shoes and pants. She was feeling strange and muzzy-headed as she started to get back into bed. Then a thought crept into her mind and lodged there. The robe was in the closet. She should put on the robe.

The robe? She had told herself she was never going to wear it again.

Because a strange sense of purpose gripped her, she walked to the closet and fumbled through the hangers. When her fingers closed over the shoulder of the garment, she sighed with relief and pleasure. Pulling it off the hanger, she shoved her arms through the sleeves, then quickly fastened the buttons.

The robe seemed to hold her in an embrace, heating

her skin, soothing her soul in a way that she was at a loss to explain. She felt as if she had come home, come back to herself.

Gratefully she tottered to the bed, crawled in and pulled the covers up to her chin. Within moments she was sleeping soundly.

The fates let her rest for a while. Then she awoke. Not in the here and now, but in another woman's life—the woman she had visited twice before. She was Linette again, standing in the garden patch outside her cabin, looking toward the bayou, watching the rain fall, waiting for her love.

As Linette, she knew Andre had been in New Orleans, making arrangements. He had said he would come back for her. But he had been gone for days, and now she was worried about him.

She had secretly packed some of her belongings. Her fate was out of her hands now. All she could do was wait.

Sometimes she thought it was better if he simply went away and left her here. She had a little of the second sight that her aunt possessed, and she kept thinking that something terrible was going to happen if she went away with Andre.

But if he came, she knew she would be helpless to do anything but follow her heart. She loved him and wanted to make a home for him. Do all the things a wife could do for her husband. Have his children. Grow old with him.

She was heading back inside when the sound of horses' hooves outside made her go rigid.

Looking out the window, she saw a stallion come out of the bayou. She knew the animal, knew the rider. It was Andre on Richelieu.

By the time she reached him, he had dismounted and tied the reins to the branch of a pine tree. She flew toward him, and he caught her in his arms. She melted against him as he gathered her close. The rain was falling on them, and he moved her under the shelter of the branches.

"I'm sorry, angel. I'm sorry I took so long. But I wanted to make sure we could leave New Orleans as soon as we arrived in town. There's a ship down at the docks waiting for us. We're going to San Francisco. We can live there."

"San Francisco. That's so far away. Are you sure?" she whispered.

He tightened his hold on her, then set her away from him so he could look into her eyes. "Yes. I've made all the arrangements. I sent inquiries to several cities, and one of the universities offered me a job so we don't have to worry about that. And I have some good ideas for books I want to write." He dragged in a breath and let it out in a rush. "You haven't changed your mind, have you?"

"I want to be with you," she breathed. "I haven't changed my mind about that."

"But?" he pressed.

"I'm frightened," she said in a small voice.

"Of what? Your family? My father? I'm taking you where they can never touch us. And we'll be free to love each other."

"I know. You're so smart. I could never have planned something like this in secret."

He laughed. "No. You're too honest. Too straightforward."

She was hardly listening. "I don't know what you see in me."

"I love you. I look at you, and I see all the good, warm, gentle things that I never had in my life until I met you."

"Oh, Andre." She lifted her arms, bringing his head down to hers. As soon as his lips met hers, she felt a profound sense of relief. How could she be worried? He was holding her and kissing her as though he had been starving for the taste of her, and she felt the same.

She opened for him, feasting from him, thinking that no one was home and she could take him into the house, into her bedroom. She wanted him. They would be married soon, but there was no reason to wait for the joy of making love with him.

Before she had drunk her fill, he lifted his lips, leaving her light-headed. "We have to go," he said, his voice thick.

She knew he was right.

"Are you ready? Or do you need some time to get your things together?"

"I'm almost ready." She went back into the cabin and brought out the small bag she had already packed. She had known she couldn't take much on horseback, so she had chosen carefully. Her robe lay across the chair, and she stroked her fingers over the silky fabric. She loved the robe and would have liked to take it, but she needed other things more.

A step behind her made her turn. Andre had come into the room. He walked to her, touched the robe. "You must be a sexy sight wearing that. I'd like to see it."

She flushed.

"I'll get you one you'll love even more."

"You don't have to buy me things."

"It will be my pleasure to buy you things. You're going to be my wife. But we must go."

"Yes," she answered, her fear leaping up inside her again. She ignored the bad feelings, telling herself she was just nervous about leaving everything she had ever known to go off with Andre Gascon and feeling bad about her parents, who would be sad and angry. Maybe later when she wrote to them and told them how happy she was, they would forgive her.

Maybe they would understand how much Andre meant to her. She trusted him with her life. When he was with her, she couldn't believe that anything bad would happen.

She put a few more things into her bag, took her rain slicker from the peg by the door and followed him out of the house. He helped her up onto the broad back of Richelieu, then climbed up behind her, holding her in one arm as he started down the road that led first to St. Germaine and then to New Orleans.

She leaned against him, reassured by his strong arm looped around her waist. When she snuggled into his embrace, he bent to stroke his lips against the side of her face.

"Soon we won't have to sneak around. We won't have to run away. We'll be together always."

"Oui," she answered, closing her eyes, letting his soothing words lull her.

They were several miles from her house when she heard a roaring noise. She knew what it was. A sudden flood cannonballing through the bayou.

In back of her Andre cursed, then kicked his heels into the horse's sides. "Come on, boy. Get us out of this," he shouted as he flicked the reins.

But it was already too late. She saw a wall of water rushing toward them. Her scream was drowned out as the water hit Richelieu, sweeping both of them off the horse's broad back and into the current.

"Linette! I'll get you, Linette!" Andre cried out.

She reached toward him, but the water swept her away, and terror engulfed her as the current pulled her under.

A TERRIBLE, SICK, SCARED FEELING gripped Morgan's chest as she woke. At first she had no idea where she was. Blinking, she looked around, and the bedroom at Belle Vista came into focus in the dim light. But it was hard to anchor herself to that reality. She was still back in the dream, in the past, feeling the water grab her and sweep her away.

It was impossible to stop herself from shaking as she sat up, then gathered up a handful of the sheet to try and ground herself.

"Oh, God. Oh, God."

The words came out as a sob, and she sat, her right hand pressing against her chest as her vision blurred.

The door flew open, and someone stepped into the room. Through the mist of tears, she saw that it was Andre. His hair was disheveled, and he looked as though he'd been tramping through the swamp all night.

"What? What's wrong?" he asked urgently. He looked around the room. "Is someone here?"

His gaze probed the shadows. Charging toward the bathroom, he threw the door open. When he found it empty, he started searching the closet.

"No," she managed to gasp out. "No one's here."

"Then what is it?"

When she could only answer with a sob, he crossed to her, easing onto the bed and taking her in his arms, stroking his hand over her back and shoulders and into her hair. The spicy aroma of his body was as comforting to her as the physical contact. "What happened? What's wrong?"

She fought to gain control of her tears because she couldn't let him think she was really in danger. At least not here. Not now.

"They were caught in a flash flood…."

His body went rigid. "Who? The missing men?"

She knew she wasn't making sense, and she struggled to correct that. "No. Linette and Andre." She dashed her hand over her face.

"You know that?" he asked in a gritty voice. "How?"

She gripped his shoulders, hoping the physical contact would help her communicate. "I saw it. I felt it! I felt her terror. I felt the water pull her under."

"No!"

"Yes. I was back there. I was her again. I was afraid something bad was going to happen. Then when he came to get me, I didn't want to believe we were in danger. Not when it felt so wonderful to be in his arms. But I should have made him wait."

"Tell me more about your dream. Not just the end. What happened before that?" he whispered, strong emotions gathering in his voice.

She tried to answer and found her own terrible sadness threatening to overcome her again.

He stroked her arms. "It's okay. Just take your time."

"It was the night they left. He'd been in New Orleans making arrangements…for them to take a boat to San Francisco."

He drew in a sharp breath. "San Francisco? That's not in any of the accounts."

"I heard him tell her," she murmured.

"I know. When I dream about that night, he tells her they're going to San Francisco."

"You've dreamed about *that* night?"

"Many times. And after. I feel his despair, his loneliness."

"Oh, Lord, how do you stand it?"

"What choice do I have? The water comes. I feel his terror. He tries to get to her, but she's out of his reach. Then he has to live fifty more years."

"I'm so sorry."

"It's part of the curse. The one the voodoo priestess put on my grandfather…on me."

She tried to form another question as his hand rubbed her shoulder, then went still. "You're wearing the robe."

"Yes. I—I felt like I had to put it on." She swallowed. "The voodoo priestess was chanting outside. I woke up after the flood swept Linette away."

"I'm so sorry. Are you all right?"

"Yes. It happened a long time ago."

"That's what I tell myself."

In the dim light of dawn, they held each other, comforted each other.

"I was worried about you," she whispered. "But there was nothing I could do besides sit here and wait. Did you find those men?"

He made an angry sound. "No. I'd like to know what's going on. I'd like to think Brevard came here to yank my chain, but he was too upset to be faking it."

The stark look on his face made her clasp her hands over his shoulders.

She ached to wipe away his pain. As Linette had done in the dream, she pressed her lips to his.

She had wanted to comfort him, to reassure him. But the touch of her mouth on his was like putting a match to dry straw. Heat flared inside her—heat she was helpless to control.

He made a needy sound as he angled his head so he could feast on her mouth—the way the Andre in the dream had feasted on Linette.

Linette had been a virgin. Morgan knew what she was doing as she lay back on the bed, taking Andre with her, rolling to her side so she was lying half on top of him.

As her hands moved over him, he did the same, stroking, caressing, arousing.

Panting, she broke the kiss for a moment. "You need to take off your clothes."

"The dream turned you on."

She pressed her fingers to his lips. "No. The dream made me so sad. They never got to make love, but we can."

"That's not a good reason," he grated.

"It wouldn't be if it were the only reason." She was tired of arguing with him. It had been a long time since she had wanted to be with a man like this. But if she knew anything in her heart, it was that she wanted to make love with Andre Gascon, urgently.

"This isn't a dream. It's reality," she murmured as her hand slid down his body, finding the hard shaft of his erection behind the fly of his jeans. When she pressed her hand over him, she felt his body jerk.

"Don't."

She laughed. "If you say you don't want me, you're going to have a hard time getting me to believe it." As she said the word *hard,* she moved her hand, making him gasp.

"Oh, Morgan. I want you so much. I wanted you before you ever arrived here."

"How?"

"As soon as I found you at Light Street, I knew."

She wasn't exactly following his logic, but it didn't matter. Her main goal was to get him to stop talking. She knew she had won the battle when his hands went to the front of her robe and began to undo the buttons. She reached to help him, and their fingers tangled.

"Let me do it," he growled. "I want the pleasure of undressing you."

"Yes." She lay back, lowering her arms to her sides, looking up at him in the dim light coming through the window. It was early in the morning, she noted with some corner of her mind. The sun would come up soon.

But the light from the bathroom let her see the way his eyes burned with passion, and that thrilled her.

He finished opening the buttons of her robe, then carefully spread the front open.

She felt shy as his gaze drank her in, shy as Linette would have felt.

"You are so beautiful," he breathed. His hand moved to touch her, to stroke tenderly across her collarbone, then move slowly, slowly downward, grazing the tops of her breasts before tracing their fullness.

He skirted her nipples, and she ached to feel the pressure of his thumbs and fingers squeezing there. When his hand slid lower to run over her ribs, she made a small sound of protest.

But he kept going, tracing a circle around her navel before sliding his fingers into the triangle of hair at the top of her legs.

She wanted him to go farther, to dip his fingers into

the hot, swollen folds of her sex, but he rolled away from her and stood up.

"Come back," she pleaded, holding out her arms to him.

"In a minute." He walked to the door, closed it and snapped the lock, and she realized she had forgotten all about making sure they had privacy. Then he strode back to the bed, pulling his shirt over his head before opening his belt buckle. When he reached the side of the bed, he unzipped the jeans, shucking them down his legs along with his underwear.

He stood over her, and she feasted her eyes on him, enjoying his wonderful, hard-muscled body, his broad chest covered with dark hair, his narrow waist and flat belly. Her gaze inevitably dropped lower, focusing on the erection that stood out from his body, proud and thick.

"You are so sexy looking," she whispered.

"I was thinking the same thing."

When she realized she was still wearing the robe, she shrugged out of it, tossing it to the end of the bed.

They were both naked when he came down beside her, and her breath caught as she absorbed the wonderful sensation of his skin touching hers and the feel of his shaft pressing against her leg.

He gathered her to him, rocking with her, his hand stroking over her back and lower to caress the curve of her bottom.

"Your skin is like silk," he murmured, his fingers trailing up again, then stroking the underside of her breasts.

"I need that. More of that," she gasped out, taking his hands and pressing them against her nipples.

"I need it, too," he answered, taking the engorged tips between his fingertips and squeezing them gently. "Does that feel good?"

"Yes. I want everything you're willing to give me."

She had denied herself this pleasure for so long. No man had touched her body with sexual intent in years. Now all the needs she had told herself were dead forever surged up to overwhelm her.

When he tugged at her nipples and rolled them between his fingers, she sobbed out her pleasure. When his mouth replaced one of his hands, sucking one hardened bud into his mouth and teasing it with his tongue and teeth, she went frantic, cupping the back of his head in her hands as she pressed her lower body against his. The sudden burst of feelings was too much for her to contain. Need spiraled out of control. She should have been prepared, but orgasm took her by surprise, rocketing through her like a shooting star flashing to earth, and she cried out with the strength of her release.

For long moments she could do nothing more than allow the storm to rage through her body.

When she could speak again, she whispered "I'm sorry" as she pressed her face against his shoulder.

He stroked her shoulder, kissed her hair, then tipped her face up so that she had to meet his questioning gaze.

"For what?"

"For…jumping the gun," she managed to say.

He laughed. "I think there's more where that came from."

She started to say that there probably wasn't more. But when his finger rubbed lightly over her still-sensitive breast, she gasped.

"Oh!"

"Yes. Much more, I think."

He brought his mouth back to hers, kissing her as though they were just getting started. His mouth moved over hers and his hands teased and tantalized, and Morgan felt him building her arousal all over again.

This time she wasn't so frantic, and the sensation of heat coursing through her was delicious.

Then his hand slid downward again, giving her most intimate flesh a quick, tantalizing brush. She arched against him, and he dipped into her sex for long, lingering strokes that pushed her toward another orgasm.

"I want you in me this time," she whispered, her fingers closing around his wonderfully hard erection.

"Oh, yes."

She lay back, guiding him to her, and they both sighed out in pleasure as he slipped inside her.

He looked down at her, his eyes dark with passion and so many other emotions that she could barely breathe.

"I've waited so long for this," he said.

"You just met me a few days ago."

He stroked her hair back from her face. "It doesn't feel like it, does it?"

"No," she admitted in a low voice. In truth, she felt as if she had known him forever. That she had been waiting for this forever.

When he began to move, she moved with him. Her ecstasy spiraled quickly. Out of control and over the moon. This time when she came, he was with her, calling out her name as his body went rigid above hers.

She floated back to earth slowly, making a small sound of protest as he moved off her. But he only came down beside her on the bed, gathering her close, kiss-

ing the side of her face while she stroked her fingers
through his hair. She was limp with pleasure, more relaxed than she had been in years, she thought.

ANDRE HELD MORGAN in his arms, watching her eyes
drift closed. She fit so well against him. It was heaven
just to hold her. Making love with her had felt like
magic. And he needed magic. So much.

Before she'd come here, he'd felt free to joke with
her. Tease her. He'd loved every scrap of herself that
she'd shared.

She'd traveled all over the world, while he'd never
traveled far from this patch of southern Louisiana, yet
it had felt like they'd had a lot in common. They liked
the same music, good food, nature and they were both
down-to-earth in a fundamental way. And their values
matched so well.

He'd been delighted to discover all those things and
more. He'd pictured the two of them sitting in the sun-
room or on the patio, talking for hours, then reaching
for each other. But when she'd arrived, everything had
changed. He'd been terrified that she would turn away
from Andre Gascon in person. Worse, he knew that he'd
dragged her into a situation more dangerous than he'd
imagined.

He hadn't known how to deal with her or with his
fears. But she hadn't allowed him to shut himself away
from her, and for that he was profoundly grateful.

She'd forced him to tell her about the curse—some
of it, at least. But there was more he had to reveal, and
more he must ask of her. But not until she knew him better.

When she did, would she run screaming from him?

Fear leaped inside him. The idea of losing her was too much to bear.

Closing his eyes, he held her in his arms, profoundly grateful for these hours of intimacy, but praying that she would stay with him even when she knew the worst about him.

He had never spent the night with a woman. Never slept with a lover in his arms. But he was glad to do it now, overwhelmed by the luxury of sharing a bed with Morgan Kirkland—not just to make love but to sleep beside her.

He drifted into the most peaceful slumber he could remember, his shoulder touching Morgan's, his leg pressed to hers.

A few hours later the sound of a car engine and angry shouting outside made his eyes snap open.

Oh, Lord, he thought, not again.

Chapter Twelve

Looking to his right, Andre saw Morgan staring wide-eyed at him as men's angry voices shattered the warm mood of the bedroom.

She sat up, exposing her beautiful breasts. When she saw him staring at her, she dragged up the sheet, and he marveled that she was thinking of modesty. Or maybe she was right. Maybe the uninvited guests in the front hall would come pounding up the stairs and burst into the bedroom. That thought had him scrambling out of bed and searching for the clothing that he'd left scattered around the room.

"What's going on?" Morgan asked.

"I don't know," he answered, as he thrust one foot into a pant leg, then the other. Still, he had a good idea of what he was going to hear, if he made it downstairs. Someone had found another body out in the bayou. Another man killed by a large cat.

He could hear the front door rattling, then footsteps hurrying across the hall. The door opened, and Janet was speaking to someone.

He had pulled on his jeans and T-shirt and saw Morgan doing the same.

"Stay here," he tossed over his shoulder as he scuffed his feet into his shoes. He was thinking that he was probably wasting his breath by giving Morgan Kirkland orders. One of the basic things he'd learned about her was that she did what she thought best. He could only thank the Lord that she'd had sense enough to stay out of the bayou last night.

As he dashed from the room, she followed a few paces behind. When he reached the bottom of the stairs, he found Janet standing against the wall, pushed to the side by a crowd of men—Sheriff Jarvis, Dwight Rivers, Bob Mansard. And Rick Brevard. Relief flooded through Andre when he saw Rick standing there. He was one of the missing men, but he was apparently alive and well.

The feeling of relief evaporated like water on a scalding griddle as Jarvis got right to the point. "Where were you last night?" he demanded.

"Why do you want to know?" Andre asked.

"Because Henri Dauphin is dead," Jarvis said, his voice flat.

Morgan stepped up beside Andre and put a hand on his arm. "If you're here, I suppose you suspect Andre. He was here all night," she said in a firm voice. "With me."

All eyes shot to her. From the way the crowd was looking at her, it was pretty clear that they knew Morgan Kirkland and Andre Gascon had just climbed out of bed. The question was how long they'd been there.

Apparently, Jarvis had already considered that line of inquiry. "All night?" he asked, tipping his head to one side, looking her up and down, taking in her tousled hair, rumpled clothing and sleepy face.

She kept her face turned toward the sheriff, and Andre waited to see if she was going to back down on the lie.

"Yes. All night," she answered.

"So you're doing more out here than just cataloging the books in the library?"

"My personal relationship with Mr. Gascon is none of your business," she said.

"It is when it's tangled up with a murder investigation."

"You're saying Henri Dauphin was murdered," she asked carefully.

Rick Brevard answered. "Yeah. I was there. I couldn't see nothin', but I heard a big cat growl. Heard Henri scream. Heard the claws tearing at him."

"But you didn't see anything?" she clarified, her voice cool and controlled. If he had ever doubted her abilities as a detective, he could see now that she was a thorough professional in her job.

"I didn't see nothin'," he admitted. "Henri, he got up to take a leak. I was in the tent."

"What were you doing camping in the bayou?" she demanded.

He looked down as he scuffed his foot against the Oriental rug, leaving a track of mud, which Janet eyed with distaste. "After we dropped the car off, we was plannin' to do some fishing."

"You mean alligator poaching, don't you?" Dwight Rivers muttered, voicing what Andre had been thinking.

"And you didn't bother telling anyone you'd be gone," Morgan clarified. "So you had people running around looking for you since you left here."

Rick looked defiant. "I don't have to tell no one my business. Anyways, that's not the point. The point is that the big cat killed Henri."

Everyone else knew where this was going. But Morgan, who had been here less than a week, asked the obvious question. "And what does that have to do with Mr.

Gascon? Are you accusing him of having a pet jaguar in the bayou?"

Andre felt his heart block his windpipe as he waited to hear how the man would answer.

The sheriff cleared his throat. "We found a leather jacket near the campsite. A jacket people in town have seen Mr. Gascon wear." He turned to Andre. "I'm going to have to take you in."

Even as he felt panic threaten to swallow him up, Andre struggled to keep his voice even. "Was the jacket worn at the elbows?" he managed to ask.

"What about it?" Jarvis said, not exactly answering the question.

"That jacket was in my SUV. I was taking it to a church sale. But with everything that's been going on out here, I didn't get a chance to drop it off."

"So you say," Jarvis answered. His voice turned hard as brass. "We'll straighten this out down at the police station."

"No!" Unable to control a spurt of panic, Andre backed away. Maybe he intended to run. Maybe not. All he knew was that he couldn't take a chance on spending the night in a jail cell. He had to stay out here at Belle Vista, where he was safe.

He realized instantly that he had made the wrong move. All at once, a gun materialized in the sheriff's hand. "Hold it right there," he said with the finality of the guy who held the winning hand. "You're coming with me."

Andre went still. In a moment of panic he had made a terrible mistake. Now he was a dead man. Or as good as dead.

As if from a long way off, he heard Morgan speaking. "You can't do this."

"I'm afraid he can," Dwight Rivers said.

The sheriff pulled Andre's hands behind his back. As if it were happening in a dream, he felt cold metal clanking around his wrists. He could hear the sheriff reciting his rights. When he was asked if he understood, he answered with a mechanical yes. He understood all right. This was the end of his life as he knew it.

His gaze shot to Morgan. There were so many things he needed to say, but he couldn't tell her any of them in front of this crowd.

"I'll get you out," she said.

All he could do was nod wordlessly, because whatever happened, it was too late now for him. For them.

As Jarvis hustled him toward the door, he saw Carl and Rick Brevard looking on in satisfaction. But Dwight Rivers didn't seem quite so gleeful. Maybe Rivers really was willing to give him the benefit of the doubt. But he wasn't the man holding the power.

Jarvis kept the gun in his hand as he hustled the prisoner to the police cruiser in the driveway. Opening the back door, he helped Andre inside, then slammed the door.

Andre looked wildly around. A metal grill separated the back seat from the front, and the door panel held no handle. The only way out of here was if Jarvis let him out, which wasn't going to happen until they arrived at the police station in St. Germaine.

By that time a crowd probably would have gathered, courtesy of Carl and Rick.

From a long way off, he heard Morgan's voice. "Sheriff," she called.

Jarvis turned to her.

"Mr. Gascon's lawyer will be in touch with you."

"You know where to find me."

The lawman walked around to the front seat and slid behind the wheel, and Andre felt his vision go black as they drove away. Morgan might think she had a way to get him out, but he was sure it wouldn't be in time.

MORGAN WATCHED the Brevard brothers swagger to their vehicle and leave. Had they stolen the jacket and planted the evidence? Or had it been Jarvis himself?

Dwight Rivers lingered. "Sorry," he said.

"About what?" Morgan snapped.

"Jarvis has been looking for an excuse to arrest him."

"On trumped-up charges."

"I hope so."

She might have stayed to talk about it; instead she charged into the house. Janet was standing in the hall, looking sick and frightened.

"It'll be all right," Morgan called to her as she sprinted down the hall to the office.

Snatching up the phone, she dialed the Light Street Detective Agency, aware of Janet watching anxiously from the doorway.

Sam Lassiter answered.

"Sam, thank God!"

"Morgan, what's wrong?" he asked as soon as he heard the panic in her voice.

"My client, Andre Gascon, has been arrested. We need Dan Cassidy down here." Dan was Sabrina's husband and a lawyer who had been a state's attorney in Baltimore. Now he worked for Light Street.

"I'll have to check his schedule."

"Clear it. This is an emergency. Andre will be in a completely hostile environment." She went on to describe what had happened, and Sam promised to get Dan down to Louisiana as soon as humanly possible. She was about to hang up when Jo O'Malley came on the line.

"I put Jason Zacharias on the job of researching the maps you faxed."

Morgan wanted to shout that she wasn't interested in the damn maps right now, but curiosity got the better of her. "He found something interesting?" she asked.

"As we guessed, they're part of a geological survey. If they're accurate, the Belle Vista property is sitting on a huge reservoir of oil. Enough oil to make someone very rich, Jason says."

Morgan whistled through her teeth. Oil. And Andre had said someone was trying to get him off his land. Could that be the reason why?

"When was the survey done?" she asked.

"Last July."

"About two months before Andre started having problems with the town," she mused. "Who commissioned the survey?"

"Jason hasn't found that out yet."

"I have to know if it was Andre or someone else."

"I'll tell you as soon as we find out," Jo promised. "Dan will be there ASAP."

That was good to know. But it didn't calm her fears as she hung up the phone.

"What survey? What are you talking about?" Janet asked.

Could she trust the housekeeper? Morgan wasn't absolutely sure. Watching the woman carefully, she said, "Apparently there's a large deposit of oil on the Belle Vista property."

Janet looked startled.

"Do you think that's why someone in town wants Andre out of here?"

"Andre can't leave," Janet whispered. "He...he can't spend the night away from here."

"The curse." Morgan swore. All roads led back to the curse. "You think the curse got him arrested?"

"Yes," Janet answered.

"Then we'll break it."

Janet looked at her with such undisguised hope in her eyes that Morgan had to turn away.

IN THE BACK of the police car, Andre silently stared at the scenery passing outside the window. This was the familiar landscape of his life, but he saw it only in a blur of green and brown. A heron took flight from the bank of a shallow pond and flapped across the marsh, soaring away from the speeding car.

Andre watched it disappear into a clump of marsh grass. It was free. He was in the back of a police car, speeding toward his doom. And there was nothing he could do about it.

Or was there?

Despite what the town thought of him, he'd never broken the law. Strange as it seemed, he'd never even gotten a speeding ticket. But now he began making desperate plans.

His heart was pounding so hard that he thought it would break through the wall of his chest. All he knew was that he couldn't let them lock him up. And he could think of only one alternative. A risky alternative.

In the next few minutes he could end up dead. If he did, maybe that was for the best.

No, not the best. If he died, whoever had framed him for the murders in the swamp would win. Though he couldn't bear that thought, he had to take a chance on getting away.

Resolve firmed his jaw. He scanned the flat marshes on either side of the road. This patch of Louisiana was as familiar to him as the contours of his own body. He knew where there was dry land. Knew where a man might suddenly break through the surface of what seemed like solid ground into thick muck. Knew where trails led into the bayou.

The car slowed as the sheriff came to the highway leading into town. Andre tensed. It was now or never.

He glanced at the bristly hairs on the back of the sheriff's neck, thinking that was part of why he'd called the guy Old Razorback. Putting that stray thought out of his mind, Andre made a strangled exclamation and fell sideways onto the seat, drumming his feet against the seat in front of him as he went down, so that the sheriff wouldn't miss the performance.

Jarvis hit the brake, then glanced around. "What's wrong?"

Andre answered with a gurgling sound in his throat. "Can't breathe…need…" He stopped talking as though his breath had suddenly been cut off while he thrashed around on the seat.

Alarm colored the sheriff's voice. "Gascon?"

Andre moaned. The grillwork between the front and back seats obscured his line of sight, but he could feel the man's gaze on him, evaluating the situation.

He lay on the seat, eyes slitted, pretending to gasp for breath, wondering on the level of gullibility he could count on from a small-town sheriff. Hopefully the handcuffs gave him that extra edge. Or maybe this wouldn't work at all. Maybe Jarvis would simply keep driving into town and tell the nice folks in St. Germaine that they'd gotten rid of a nasty problem, because it looked like the prisoner had died in the back of the patrol car. What a pity.

Andre felt every cell in his body sizzle as Jarvis

pulled to the side of the road. When he jumped out, Andre slowly released the breath he'd been holding.

It was a struggle to lie there, limp and still, as Jarvis flung the back door open.

When the sheriff leaned into the back seat, Andre jackknifed his legs, striking the lawman square in the stomach. Jarvis flew backward, coming down on his butt on the muddy shoulder of the road.

Andre sprang out of the cruiser, ducking low as he jumped into the ditch. With his hands cuffed behind his back, he almost lost his balance, but he righted himself, scrambled up the sides of the ditch and started running.

Behind him, he could hear scuffling noises. Worse, he saw a pickup truck pulling to a stop.

Merde! The Brevard brothers were in back of the patrol car.

Andre didn't wait to find out what was happening behind him, but he could hear feet pounding on the blacktop.

"Stop or I'll shoot."

Andre kept running. Into the tangle of bayou country that he had known all his life. He swerved to the right to avoid a patch of marshy ground where the mud would slow him down.

Just as he changed directions, the unmistakable whistle of a bullet went flying over his head.

"Stop, damn you," Jarvis shouted. "Don't make this worse than it already is."

Another voice drowned out the sheriff. "Stop, you bastard." That was one of the Brevards. Andre didn't know which one, and he didn't care.

He had no choice about what he was doing. No choice at all. He kept going, almost falling as he crossed a patch of slick ground, then righting himself as he made for the safety of the low branches of a small holly tree.

The first bullet had been a warning. The next one was meant to bring down the fugitive. It whistled past his shoulder and plowed into a nearby tree trunk. But Andre kept going, running awkwardly with his hands behind his back, knowing that no man would dare follow him into the snake- and alligator-infested swamp.

He stumbled, then got his balance and kept going, splashing through a trough of water. The vegetation closed around him, and he breathed out a sigh. He was safe—for the moment.

Escaping had been his only choice, as there was no way he could let the sheriff lock him in a cell overnight. Still, he knew his action had confirmed his guilt in the eyes of his enemies. And his hands were still cuffed. What the hell was he going to do about that, out in the wilderness where a man needed a fighting chance against the dangers lurking on all sides?

Chapter Thirteen

Morgan went back to her room and put on a clean shirt, thinking that she could go into town and make it clear that she was supporting Andre—even if that wouldn't do her much good until Dan Cassidy arrived.

She had just reached the front hall, when the sound of cars roaring up the driveway made her whole body go rigid. The sheriff and the angry men had left ten minutes ago. Now what was happening?

Quickly she threw open the front door.

She goggled when she saw the police car was back, then allowed herself to feel a spurt of hope. Maybe Sheriff Jarvis was finally admitting that he'd made a mistake and was bringing Andre home.

When she saw the pickup with the Brevards trailing along behind him, she was more confused than ever. Her heart was pounding as she ran down the steps and looked into the back seat of the cruiser. It was empty.

A feeling of sick panic rose in her throat.

"What happened?" she gasped out. "Where's Andre?"

"The bastard escaped," Jarvis answered.

"Oh, God. How?"

"Assaulting a police officer."

She stared at him. "You mean you?"

"Who the hell else?" he snapped.

She shook her head in denial. Andre was too logical, too disciplined for that. "He couldn't have."

The Brevards joined the sheriff in the driveway. "Maybe you don't think so, but we saw it. He kicked Sheriff Jarvis in the stomach, then went tear-assing into the swamp. If that don't prove he's guilty, nothin' does."

"He's not," she whispered, trying to figure out what had happened. All she knew was that Andre must have been desperate. Had the sheriff threatened him? She stared at the man. His face was red, his trooper pants were streaked with mud, and he wouldn't meet her eyes, but she couldn't be sure what any of that proved.

As she stood there wondering what to do, the man brushed past her and climbed one of the curving staircases, then yanked open the front door without bothering to knock. Janet dashed into the front hall.

"What are you doing back here?" she gasped out.

"Looking for a fugitive."

"Who?"

"Gascon. Your employer has escaped."

Janet's eyes shot to Morgan, who nodded in confirmation.

Jarvis clumped across the front hall and started up the stairs, while the Brevards charged up the exterior steps toward the door.

Janet blocked their way. "You trash, hold it right there. You have no call to come in here," she shouted, and slammed the door in their faces.

Morgan could hear them cursing on the front landing as she and Janet trailed the sheriff to the second floor of the house. He began striding down the hall, opening doors as though he was the master of the plantation.

"You can't do that! You don't have a search warrant," Morgan called after him.

His pace didn't slacken. "I don't need a search warrant. Like I said, I'm in hot pursuit of a fugitive from justice."

That might be technically true. But did Jarvis really think Andre had mucked his way through the swamp and back here faster than a car and truck could drive?

That wasn't logical. Apparently the sheriff was using the opportunity to do some snooping around. When he got to her room, he threw open the door, then stood staring at the tangled sheets before looking back at her. She wanted to tell him that what had happened in the bedroom was none of his business. Instead she kept her hands at her sides.

"Touch any of my personal things, and you'll hear from my lawyer," she growled.

He stopped in the act of reaching for the lid of the suitcase that sat on a low table, then brushed past her and continued down the hall, opening more doors into bedrooms that Morgan hadn't seen.

All of the rooms were beautifully furnished, decorated in an old-world style. Most, though, were impersonal, as if they were waiting for someone to inhabit them.

Two rooms were different. One appeared to belong to a woman. An antique mirror and brush set sat on the dresser, and several paperback romance novels were piled beside the bed. The closet door was open, and Morgan could see dresses that Janet had worn on previous occasions.

Jarvis turned to the housekeeper. "Your room?"

"Yes," she answered in a strained voice.

"And she'd appreciate it if you removed yourself from it," Morgan said.

"The fugitive could be in here."

"You think he somehow got back to the house before you did?" Morgan couldn't stop herself from snapping.

"I'm not making any assumptions," Jarvis said mildly.

"And if I ask you to wait for Mr. Gascon's lawyer?" she asked.

"I'd say you'd be hindering my investigation."

Morgan had conducted enough illegal searches in her time to know why the sheriff was taking this opportunity. Since she couldn't physically bar him from the house, she followed him down the hall to the last bedroom on the right.

It was much different from any of the others they'd entered. Obviously a man's private sanctuary, it contained a large dark dresser and chest, the fronts accentuated by bold carving details. Across from the dresser was a wide bed.

Floor-to-ceiling shelves occupied the short wall next to the bathroom. Although Morgan objected to the sheriff's being in here, she couldn't hold back her own curiosity as she scanned book titles and looked at the old black-and-white photographs.

The people in the prints looked as if they were related to Andre. In one, a small boy of around two or three stood between an attractive woman and a man who stood stiffly as he stared at the camera.

She and Jarvis both looked more closely. The boy could be Andre. He stood close to his mother. The woman had her arm around him, but there was an uncertain expression on her face, as though she wasn't sure she belonged in the photo.

Jarvis yanked open the closet. Men's clothing hung neatly inside, shirts and slacks arranged by color, and the aroma that clung to them was the aroma that she associated with Andre.

The bathroom smelled like him, too. On the sink sat a razor, along with aftershave, a toothbrush in a glass and other evidence that the room was used by a man—specifically Andre Gascon. And that he was compulsively neat and orderly about his personal belongings.

Over on a side counter, however, was something that made her eyes widen. She saw a hot plate with a small pot on the burner.

Jarvis saw it at the same time and charged across the room. When he lifted the lid, the pungent aroma wafted into the room—the same aroma that she'd caught on Andre's skin.

"What's this?" Jarvis growled.

"I don't know. An herb extract?" she improvised.

"Or drugs. I'm taking this with me."

Containing her own consternation, she said, "Wait a minute. You can't do that. He's not hiding in that pot. So if you're looking for evidence of a crime, you'd better come back with a warrant."

The sheriff went rigid, then slammed the top back on the pot. "Right," he growled. "But he may come back here to get this stuff."

He strode toward the bed, looking at the neatly made surface. "He didn't sleep here."

She kept her head tipped up. "I told you—he was with me. All night."

When Janet went to say something, Morgan shook her head, and the housekeeper's features closed up.

Jarvis addressed both of them. "You'd better let me know if he shows up."

Neither of them made a sound.

"No. Scratch that. I don't trust you to do the right thing. I'm sending a couple of deputies out here. If he comes back, we'll get him."

Morgan knew she should keep her mouth shut, but she couldn't hold back the words that sprang to her lips. "What's going on with you, Sheriff? Did the guys in town feed you a bunch of wild stories about Andre Gascon? Is that it? You think if you arrest him—or shoot him—that will solve all the problems in St. Germaine?"

"I don't have to discuss this case with you!"

"You'll have to discuss it with Mr. Gascon's lawyer."

"Yeah, maybe his lawyer will explain why he ran away." His gaze drilled into her. "And if you go one beat further, I'll arrest you for verbal assault."

Knowing he could do it, Morgan clamped her jaw shut. There was a lot more she wanted to say. She wanted to ask what the sheriff really thought about the murders in the bayou. If a jaguar was killing people, what did that have to do with Andre's jacket? Jarvis couldn't make a case out of that. But what if the town was so out of control that Andre never reached trial?

Since she hadn't completely lost her sanity, she didn't ask any of those questions.

Jarvis strode out of the room and down the hall. They heard him descending the steps. Long moments ticked by before the front door slammed shut. Still, Morgan went to the landing and looked over. In their absence, the pickup had departed, and as they watched, Jarvis revved the cruiser and pulled away.

Morgan looked back at Janet. "What was in that pot?" she asked, hearing the strained tone of her voice.

"Like you said, herbs."

"For what?"

"For his allergies."

She wanted to demand a better answer. She wanted to know if Andre was brewing drugs. Instead she hit Janet with another question. "You said last night you had the second sight."

Janet nodded.

"What does that mean?"

"That sometimes I…know things."

"Do you know where Andre went?"

"No."

"Does he have someplace in the swamp where he sleeps?"

The housekeeper's face contorted. "How do you know he sleeps there?"

"If he spends the night outside, he has to sleep somewhere."

"He goes deep into the bayou. I don't know if he has a special place," she allowed. "And if he did, you wouldn't be able to find it."

"Well, he's handcuffed and in trouble. If you can tell me where he is, you have to do it."

"If I had any idea, I'd tell you, child. But he knows his way around. He'll be okay."

"Maybe he would if his hands were free," Morgan answered. She ached to go to him. If she had a hacksaw, she could cut the chain between the cuffs. But she didn't have a clue where to find him.

She gave Janet a direct look. "Okay, you go down and act as normal as you can."

The housekeeper headed for the stairs.

Morgan went back into her room and closed the door. Fighting the tight feeling in her chest, she called Light Street, hoping she could catch Dan before he left so he'd know what kind of situation he was walking into.

Jo O'Malley took her call.

"What's wrong?" she asked, obviously picking up on Morgan's tone of voice.

She swallowed. "We've had an...unfortunate development."

"Better spit it out."

"Andre escaped from the sheriff. He's hiding out in the bayou."

"Not good," Jo murmured.

"I know. But he's not guilty," she added quickly.

"He's made himself look like he is."

"You don't have to tell me that," Morgan snapped, then made an effort to calm her voice, since her anger wasn't directed at her boss. "I called to tell Dan what happened and ask him to come straight to the house rather than stopping in town."

"He's already on his way to the airport. We're flying him down in the Randolph Security Gulfstream, so there are no restrictions on calling him en route. Just a minute, let me get his cell phone number."

Morgan copied down the number. She was about to hang up when Jo said, "Do I detect that you're getting emotionally involved with your client?"

The question sent a shock wave through Morgan. She'd hoped that Jo wouldn't zero in on the personal aspect of her distress. Apparently her friend was tuned in enough to read between the lines of the conversation very well.

Morgan sighed. She might have denied it, but it felt like a relief to admit, "I guess you can say that."

"You trust him?" Jo asked sharply.

Again, her friend was picking up more from the conversation than Morgan was actually saying. "I want to," she whispered.

Jo cleared her throat. "When you came to us, you were so closed up. It sounds like you're letting someone into your life again. I just wish I were down there so I could meet him. But I can't. So I'll just say that if he hurts you, I'll tear him apart."

Morgan couldn't repress a small laugh. "Thanks—I think."

"Be careful," Jo ordered. "I mean be careful of those small-town cops. And be careful of yourself. Or is it too late to give you that warning?"

"It may be too late," Morgan whispered, then changed the subject. "I'd better get off and call Dan."

"He should be there in a couple of hours."

"Jo, thanks." Next, Morgan had a quick conversation with the lawyer. Then, after putting down the phone, she paced restlessly up and down the length of her room, frustration bubbling inside her.

She couldn't just sit here and wait for the men from the sheriff's department to take over the estate. If she wanted to do something constructive without anyone tracking her movements, it had better be soon.

Exchanging her tennis shoes for hiking boots, she stuffed her gun inside her knapsack. She was about to leave her room when she stopped. Going back to her luggage, she took out a bulletproof vest and put it on.

To conceal its bulkiness, she pulled out the leather jacket that she hadn't needed since she'd arrived.

With the protection in place, she headed for the back stairs.

Janet was standing at the counter, kneading bread. Morgan stopped. Making bread was such a strange thing to be doing at a time like this that Morgan found herself staring at the woman, trying to figure out if she'd lost her mind.

Janet lifted her head so Morgan could see the desperation on her face. And suddenly she understood better.

"I guess that helps calm you," she said.

"Yes," Janet answered grimly. "I love to cook. When anything worries me, I come into the kitchen and start pounding dough and beating batter."

She peered at Morgan. "Child, what are you wearing?"

"I was feeling cold," Morgan answered. "And I'm not so calm either, so I'm going out to have a look around before the boys in blue get here."

"Is that safe?"

"I don't know but I can't just sit inside." She hesitated for a moment. "If I'm not back in an hour, call my office." Walking across the kitchen, she wrote the Light Street number on the pad of paper beside the phone.

"You should stay in. You'll broil in that outfit."

"I have to go out." Turning, she cleared her throat. "Do we have a large hunk of meat I could take with me?" she asked.

Janet's eyebrows lifted "Why?"

"I need it for bait."

Janet gave her a long look. "I guess I have to assume you haven't gone off the deep end of the dock."

"I hope not."

The housekeeper nodded. "I was planning to have a beef roast for dinner. I'm certainly not going to serve it to those deputies."

"I believe I can put it to better use." Morgan took the meat from the refrigerator, relieved that the housekeeper wasn't asking more pointed questions. Sliding the roast into a plastic grocery bag, she stuffed the whole thing into her knapsack, then stepped into the humid afternoon. Her first stop was the potting shed, where she snatched up the long pruning pole designed for snipping off tree branches that were too high to reach from the ground.

Then she lifted a heavy bolt cutter off its hook. If the deputies were on the property when she got back, she might have to leave the cutters in the swamp. That would probably make Andre angry when he came back.

When he came back. A sob sneaked up on her, and she struggled to keep it locked behind her lips as she hurried out of the shed and closed the door behind her.

With her equipment in tow, she made for the swampy area beyond the lawn, heading toward the small river that had stopped her progress into the swamp the first day she'd explored the estate.

She stepped into the shadows under the trees, feeling the temperature of the humid air drop several degrees. She'd intended to go directly to the island; instead she hesitated for a moment, then detoured in the direction of the road. When she was well into the tangle of underbrush, she called out softly, "Andre? Are you there, Andre?"

She held her breath, listening for an answer—or for the sound of leaves crackling. But the swamp was silent except for the buzzing of insects.

"Why did you run?" she asked.

Again only the insects answered.

"It must have been for a good reason, otherwise you wouldn't have taken the chance," she said, hoping she could convince him that she was on his side.

But nobody replied. She might have been talking to herself, and she wanted to scream in frustration. Jo was right; she had become emotionally involved in a very short period of time. After two years of feeling dead she was finally alive again.

"Don't you trust me?" she demanded, her temper rising. Then she told herself that getting mad at him wasn't going to do either one of them any good. And really, he could be miles from here and totally unable to hear her.

She gave the conversation one more try. "I brought a bolt cutter. At least let me cut your handcuffs apart," she offered.

When the silence lengthened, she sighed and walked back toward the river.

The sun had gone behind a cloud. Below the thick canopy of trees, the bayou was dark and forbidding. A shiver traveled over her skin as she looked down at the dark water.

Her friend the alligator was waiting near the make-shift bridge, looking loglike and innocent. But she wasn't fooled. She had seen him in action before.

Opening her knapsack, she took out the roast Janet had given her, then pulled off the plastic covering. When she held it over the water, the alligator stirred.

"Come and get your dinner," she called, waving the meat, then tossing it into the water. It landed with a splash, and immediately the alligator went after it, diving below the surface in search of her offering.

From the creature's behavior, she knew that whoever had been coming to the island had been feeding the gator, keeping it here to do guard duty.

Well, now the guard dog was otherwise engaged.

A satisfied smile flickered around her lips as she stepped up onto the log. The pole she'd used the first time had been too short, but this one was long enough to work. She set it carefully into the water, then took a step forward, before moving the pole to the next spot. She knew what to expect—on the log and below the surface of the water—and since she didn't have to worry about the alligator, she could focus on what she was doing.

Using the longer pole and relying on the traction of her hiking boots, she worked her way slowly but surely across the log. It was still slippery, but her preparations had paid off. After five nerve-racking minutes, she reached the island and breathed out a sigh of relief.

Carefully she set down her balance pole then straightened. Standing on the island gave her a strangely creepy feeling.

Was she alone here?

Looking down, she saw definite boot prints in the mud. Someone had been to this place recently. Not just once, but several times, since there were overlapping prints in the muck.

She looked back toward the far shore. The distance from the opposite bank wasn't really all that great, but on the island, she felt isolated from the rest of the world. Which was why whoever had been over here had used the place, she told herself.

She took in a breath of soggy air. She'd been outside only a few minutes, but the leather jacket and bulletproof vest were making perspiration pour down her body.

Reaching inside her knapsack, she slipped the revolver into her hand. The weapon gave her a sense of well-being as she started forward, following the trail of footprints from the log bridge.

She wasn't sure what she was looking for, but she flicked her gaze from the ground to the foliage at shoulder level, making sure she wasn't being stalked by someone lurking in the underbrush.

The island was long and thin. As she moved farther from the log, she was able to keep one bank or the other in sight.

After walking across to the far side, she started along the length. About a hundred paces from where she'd crossed over the log, she came to a spot that looked wrong. Leaves were strewn thickly on the ground, yet something about the arrangement didn't seem natural.

Stooping down, she brushed them aside and found a camouflage trampoline. Excitement leaped inside her, but when she lifted it up, nothing was underneath.

Strange. Someone had gone to a lot of trouble to hide nothing.

She picked up a stick and poked in the dirt. It seemed compressed, not like someone had buried anything.

Just then, thunder rumbled in the distance, and a few fat drops of rain splatted on the leaves above her, adding to her sense of uneasiness. She'd gotten caught in a flash flood once. She should have asked if it ever happened this close to the plantation house. Maybe a better question was: Did this island ever end up underwater?

She glanced over her shoulder, torn. She'd gone to

a lot of trouble to get over here, but now she wasn't so sure it was a great idea. Especially since the only piece of evidence she'd found turned out to be a dud.

She wanted to keep searching. This might be her last chance to do any snooping around without the deputies breathing down her neck. But she wasn't going to put herself in danger just because she was stubborn.

Retracing her steps, she started back toward the log bridge.

When she got there, she stopped short. She had lain the long pruning pole on the ground beside the bank. Now it was missing.

As she stared at the new footprints on the ground, she felt the hairs rise on the back of her neck.

Chapter Fourteen

Gun in hand, Morgan looked at the log and the water. She didn't see her friend the alligator, but that didn't mean he had gone away. He could be lurking out of sight, waiting for something more substantial than a beef roast.

Before she could decide what to do, something leaped onto her from behind, raking sharp claws down her back and tearing her jacket.

A scream tore from her throat as she tried to fight off her attacker, but something shot around her body, holding her in place. She blinked as she tried to interpret what she was seeing—a man's arm covered by a camouflage shirt. A shirt that matched the tarp she'd found on the ground.

But the shirt wasn't the important part. His hand was covered with a huge glove, and attached to the glove were long animal claws.

She tried to kick backward, but he was ready for that.

His leg shot out, tripping her, then holding her upright against his body. The gun was still in her hand, but her arm was clamped to her side, making it impossible to shoot effectively anywhere but at the ground.

The claws of her attacker's other hand raked through the fabric of her shirt. They would have torn through her skin had she not been cautious enough to wear the bulletproof vest.

The analytical part of her mind was still struggling to work. She knew that the claw marks would look like they were made by a big cat. But this was no cat holding her with one hand and raking at her chest with the other. It was a man.

She tried to twist around, but he held her in place. She tried to butt her head back, but he conked her on the back of the skull with his chin, stunning her.

"What the hell are you wearing?" a voice growled in her ear—a voice she'd heard before. But she couldn't place him now.

As she fought for her life, she heard a loud roar and the sound of something heavy landing on solid ground—then coming at her with the force of a speeding train.

Whatever it was hit her and the assailant from behind.

A gurgling sound rose in the man's throat as he tried to get away. But something held him in place. In her peripheral vision, she saw a blur of orange-and-black fur.

The jaguar had come leaping out of the bayou again. This time he hadn't kept his distance.

Yet she knew on some instinctive level that he would never hurt her. He was risking everything to save her.

As she scrambled away, he rolled the man over twice. When the assailant came faceup, she saw that it was Dwight Rivers, the head of the chamber of commerce.

"No," he screamed as he tried to fight the jaguar. "Get off me."

Then, from the edge of the swamp, she heard men shouting.

"Go," she told the cat. "Go on. Get out of here before they start shooting. I have him covered." As she spoke, she raised the gun that had been useless until now.

The jaguar could have ripped out Rivers's throat. Instead it raised its huge head and looked her in the eye, then bounded off into a thicket. Again she heard it scrambling through the foliage, then the sound of it landing on the far shore.

"Don't move," she warned Rivers, struggling to sound in control of the situation as he cowered on the ground, his shirt covered with mud and his eyes wild.

"You won't shoot me," he said, pushing himself up, then starting for the log.

"Hold it," Morgan shouted. In the background across the water she could see men coming through the trees. If she shot at Rivers, she'd risk hitting them.

As she watched helplessly, her assailant sprang onto the makeshift bridge. Halfway across, he slipped off and fell into the water.

His curse was followed by a scream as something powerful dragged him under.

The alligator.

She heard thrashing noises below the surface, saw the water roiling. His own "guard dog" had leaped on him.

Sheriff Jarvis and another man came thumping through the underbrush, arriving at the riverbank in time to see the bayou churning.

"What the hell is going on?" he demanded, eyeing her gun. "Put down your weapon."

Her heart was still pounding as she laid the gun on the ground, then turned back to face the sheriff. "Dwight Rivers just tried to kill me. I got away from him, but he's been giving snacks to an alligator under that log. When he slipped off trying to get away from me, it got him."

The water was still boiling below the log. As they peered into the murky depths, a red stain rose to the surface.

"Rivers?" Jarvis wheezed.

"Yes, Rivers. I guess he's the one who's been feeding you all those nasty stories about Andre."

"Wait a minute. What are you trying to pull? Rivers left with the rest of us," Jarvis muttered.

"That's what he wanted you to think. When you find his body, you'll see he's got on leather gloves with big claws. He's the one who's been killing people out in the bayou and making it look like a jaguar did it."

Jarvis looked at her as though he couldn't wrap his head around that scenario.

Morgan stood up and held out her arms, then turned around, displaying the huge claw marks shredding her jacket and her shirt. "It wasn't an animal that did this," she said in a calm voice that belied the emotions roiling inside of her. "It was Rivers. He raked me pretty good. I'd be mauled to death by now if I weren't wearing a bulletproof vest."

"You expect me to take your word that it was him?"

"I expect you to find enough of him to see the gloves and the claws. I imagine the alligator isn't going to eat them."

Jarvis still regarded her with skepticism. "How did you get away?" he asked.

Morgan had a split second to decide on her answer.

"He wasn't expecting me to be wearing any kind of body protection. I was able to fight him, then get my gun into position."

"But you didn't shoot him?"

"If I'd shot at him, I would have risked hitting you."

The sheriff answered with a guttural sound, then spoke into the microphone attached to his collar, asking for a team from the morgue to find what was left of Rivers's body.

"Can you help me back across? I had a long pole to lean on when I came over, but I think he threw it in the water."

The man with Jarvis pulled down a dead branch and held it out to her. Grasping it tightly, she made her way back across, then breathed out a sigh as she stepped onto solid ground.

"What were you doing over there?"

"I found this place a few days ago. I saw boot prints on the log and on the ground. I figured someone had been over there. I wanted to know what they were hiding."

"Well, this is Gascon's property."

"Right. And someone has been watching the house. I found a bunch of cigarette butts on the ground."

"Where are they?"

"Unfortunately, I think Rivers knew I discovered them, so he cleaned up after himself."

She stepped away from the bank. "I'd like to go back to the house and change my torn clothing, if you don't mind."

Jarvis might have objected, but the rain that had been threatening began to fall, and she took off quickly through the trees.

Janet was standing on the back porch, anxiously following her progress across the lawn.

"What happened?" the housekeeper demanded as she and the men climbed the steps.

"Dwight Rivers was the killer. He was wearing gloves with animal claws. But he ended up in an alligator's mouth," she said, then added, "I'll give you the whole story later."

"Where's Andre?" Janet asked.

Morgan paused in midstride, eyeing the men who had entered the kitchen and were listening with interest. Her throat constricted, but she managed to say, "I haven't seen him." Before Jarvis could say anything else, she added, "I'm going to take a shower and change. I'll talk to you later."

She saw his jaw muscles work and knew that he wanted to force her into an interview now.

"I need to get out of this bulletproof vest," she added, then pulled off her jacket and tossed it over a chair. "You'll want this for evidence," she said. While she was in a reckless mood, she also pulled off her shirt in front of the goggling men. The Kevlar vest kept her modest. "And take the shirt, too," she said, before racing for the stairs. "When you find Rivers's claws, you can match them to the scratch marks."

In her room, she slammed the door, wondering what she was going to do now. She needed time to herself, time to get her story straight, since Dwight Rivers wasn't going to contradict her.

She stared around, feeling disoriented, noting that Janet had come in and made the bed while she was gone. So what did the housekeeper think about what had happened between her and Andre?

And why should she care, Morgan asked herself. It was a logical question, but she knew that she wanted Janet on her side.

That was the least of her problems at the moment. She'd come up here to think before she spoke to Jarvis. So what was her story? What exactly had happened? She knew she wasn't going to tell the sheriff that a big cat had come leaping to her rescue, as if he cared about what happened to her. That would take too much explaining, she told herself. But deep down, she knew there was more to her reluctance to talk about the jaguar. Something she wasn't quite willing to face.

She grabbed clean clothing, then stepped into the bathroom, undressed and took her time under the hot water. Finally, when the water started to cool, she climbed out, toweled off and dressed before using the hair dryer.

As she stepped into the bedroom, her jaw fell open. She'd locked the door, but someone had opened it.

Dan Cassidy, to be exact. He was sitting in one of the chairs by the window, his leg crossed to make a writing surface as he scrawled notes on a legal pad.

"You've got some guys downstairs chomping at the bit to quiz you," he said mildly.

"You were taking a chance on my being dressed," she answered.

"Nah. Not with Jarvis in the house."

She charged across the room. When he stood, they embraced. "It's good to see a friendly face," she breathed. "Thank you for getting here so quickly."

"It sounded like you needed help," he answered in a matter-of-fact voice. Yet she could hear his concern beneath the surface. "You all right?"

"Yes."

"Hang in there. It's almost over."

"I hope so. But...but..."

"What?"

"Andre still isn't back."

"Yeah. That's a problem," Dan acknowledged. "Do you think he's aware of the developments?"

"I don't know," she answered, then asked a question of her own. "Did they recover the body from the bayou?"

"While you were in the shower. The gator took off his leg." Dan cleared his throat. "From what I understand an alligator may eat part of a body, then stow the rest for later meals. So Rivers was under a submerged log."

"Charming. What happened to the alligator?"

"He's going to augment the shoe and purse industry."

She snorted, then asked, "Speaking of hides, what about those big leather gloves with the claws that Rivers had on his hands?"

"They found them."

"Well, score one for me."

Dan took his seat again. "Fill me in on the details, starting with this morning when Jarvis came to arrest Gascon."

She dropped into the other chair and started talking.

Dan let her go at her own pace, making only a few comments and asking questions to clarify points.

She was still trying to decide what to tell him about getting away from Rivers when a commotion downstairs had both her and Dan jumping up.

Loud voices led them back to the kitchen.

When they charged into the kitchen, Andre stood by the door, muddy and matted. His gaze shot to her.

"Thank God," she said, then stopped. She had been about to rush to him and hug him, but something checked her stride. It might have been the audience. Or something more, something she couldn't deal with yet. The doubtful look in his eye didn't help.

"Are you all right?" he asked in a strained voice.

"Yes," she answered.

"You're under arrest," Jarvis interrupted, then looked at Andre's wrists. "How the hell did you get out of those handcuffs?"

"I don't know," he answered. "Someone knocked me out, and when I came to, they were gone."

Jarvis's eyes narrowed. "You expect me to believe that?"

Andre shrugged. "Believe what you want." In an almost inaudible voice, he added, "You have all along."

Jarvis's eyes flashed.

Dan stepped between the two men. "Now that we know that someone else was responsible for the murders in the bayou, what's he under arrest for?"

"Assaulting an officer," Jarvis snapped.

"You mean you arrested him because you believed Rivers's cock-and-bull story about an animal in the swamp attacking people."

"Gascon's jacket was found at the latest murder scene."

"And how does that jibe with an animal attack—unless you can prove that he's keeping a trained cat in the bayou?"

Somebody in the crowd snickered, and Jarvis whirled to glare at the man. A few hours ago they'd been willing to believe a lot of wild stories about Andre. Now it looked like some sanity was returning.

"If you take Gascon in now, I'm going to sue you for false arrest," Dan said.

The sheriff considered his words, then shifted his weight from one foot to the other.

"You made a serious mistake by arresting a man on trumped-up charges," Dan added.

"Now wait a minute—"

Dan plowed on. "If this whole story gets out, you'll be the laughingstock of the law enforcement bulletin boards."

"Are you threatening me?" Jarvis demanded.

Dan spread his hands in a gesture of innocence. "Of course not. I'm just pointing out that it's to your advantage to switch your focus. You've solved a series of murders going back several months. You proved that Dwight Rivers was clawing people to death in the backcountry. That's something to be proud of. And the community will be grateful."

The sheriff thought that over. "And what would you say was Mr. Rivers's motive for the murders?" he asked in a tight voice.

There was utter silence in the room. Then Morgan took a step forward. "He had a geological survey done of the area and found oil on Belle Vista land. He wanted to drive Mr. Gascon away. Or get him lynched," she added in a low voice.

Andre was staring at her. "How do you know that?"

"I found the geological survey maps you hid in a library book because you didn't want to deal with the consequences. I have to assume Rivers had the survey commissioned."

"He did," Dan snapped. "We've been a little busy, so I hadn't gotten around to giving you that information yet."

Jarvis looked from her to Andre. "You know there's oil on your property?"

"Yes," he admitted. "But I wasn't going to screw up the natural environment for my own profit."

"Rivers talked to you about it?" Dan asked.

"No. He stayed out of it. But a consultant from Houston came down here and gave me the information. It was handled so that I had no idea anyone in town even knew about it."

"So, you've got your motive," Dan said to Jarvis.

The sheriff nodded.

"And Andre Gascon is off the hook," Dan clarified.

When the sheriff nodded again, Morgan felt some of the tightness in her chest ease.

In the next moment the lawman focused on her. "You still haven't given me a statement."

"I can do that," she said in a weary voice.

"With her lawyer present," Dan added. "And I'd like you to do it here rather than in town. Mrs. Kirkland has been through a frightening experience, and I don't want her stressed any more than she has to be."

Jarvis made a sound of annoyance, but he agreed to let her stay at the plantation.

"You can use the den," Janet suggested.

Before Dan led her away, Morgan's eyes shot to Andre. They needed to talk. But it seemed she wasn't going to be allowed to do that yet.

She, Dan and the sheriff repaired to the den. When they had closed the door and sat down, Jarvis got out a notebook, then started with some easy questions like her name, date of birth and driver's license number. Then he hit her with something more controversial. "For the record, you're not a librarian, are you?"

She glanced at Dan. When he nodded, she said, "I'm a private detective hired by Mr. Gascon to find out who was murdering people in the swamp and trying to pin it on him."

"So you admit you were operating under false pretenses," Jarvis snapped.

She kept her gaze steady. "That's what undercover work is about."

To her relief, Jarvis didn't object to the explanation. But he didn't let her walk away, either. With more skill than she might have expected, he took her through the recent events in the bayou, with particular attention to how she had gotten away from Rivers.

Even when the lawman came at her from different angles, she stuck to her story about escaping on her own.

"So are we done?" Dan finally asked.

Morgan wanted to turn the tables and ask the sheriff some questions. She was thinking that Rivers had probably paid the man off. But she figured she'd better keep her mouth shut. She could investigate the sheriff later.

She was relieved when Jarvis said, "We're finished for now."

When he had left, Dan turned to her. "Do you want me to stay?"

"Do you think I need you?"

"I think Jarvis is satisfied with your answers."

They walked back to the kitchen, where Janet was busy washing dishes.

"Jo advised me to get a room in town," Dan said.

"Oh, she did?" Morgan asked.

"Yes. She said you and Gascon…had some issues. And you probably wouldn't want me hanging around."

Morgan didn't know whether to be grateful or upset that Jo had reported their private conversation to a third party. "How much did Jo say?" she asked.

"Not much." He cupped his hand over her shoulder and squeezed warmly. "I can see you don't need me here now. I'll talk to you in the morning."

She might have insisted that he stay at the plantation, but in truth she wanted to talk to Andre in private.

As soon as Dan and the sheriff had cleared out of the kitchen, she turned to Janet. "Where's Andre?"

"He washed up, then went out," the housekeeper answered.

"Out where?"

The woman hesitated. "To his garden patch."

"Which is where?"

Janet sighed. "I guess you're not going to allow him any more time."

"For what?"

The woman gave her a stony look.

Morgan nodded. "Right, you're not about to tell me. I have to figure it out for myself."

Janet gave her a small smile. "You're learning. Come on, I'll show you where to find him."

They stepped outside, and to her surprise, Morgan saw that the sun was already sinking low in the western sky.

Janet paused and looked at the sunset, then quickened her pace as she led the way across the back lawn. When they reached the swamp area, Morgan felt her throat close. She'd gotten into serious trouble out there. Coming back so soon hadn't been in her plans. When Janet glanced back at her, she firmed her jaw and followed.

The housekeeper gestured toward a patch of wild roses. "In there." Then she stepped around Morgan and started back to the house.

Morgan watched her leave before walking slowly toward the brambles. As she approached the screen of thorny greenery, she caught a familiar scent—the scent that she had associated with Andre.

Through the rose canes, she saw him dressed in jeans and a dark T-shirt, down on his knees, weeding a patch of low plants that had curly leaves tinged with red. He was totally focused on his work. The sight of him going about his normal routine made her heart squeeze painfully. As she stepped closer, he stopped moving, obviously aware that he was being watched.

"It's a little difficult to talk with a bramble patch between us. How do I get in there?" she asked.

Silently he stood and carefully pulled some rose canes aside, so she could step into the enclosure.

She wanted to reach out toward him, but his posture warned her not to come any closer.

"What are you doing here?" he asked.

"I could ask you the same question." She breathed in a draft of the humid air, feeling enveloped by the brambles and the scent of the plants—the scent of Andre himself.

Kneeling down, she rubbed her fingers over a curly leaf, then brought it to her nose. "What is this?" she asked sharply, wondering if he would finally tell her the truth.

"What do you think it is?"

"A drug," she shot back. "But not anything I recognize. Is that how you're making your money, growing some new illegal substance?"

He laughed. "Is that what you really think?"

"I don't know, since you won't tell me anything. But I saw your pot of leaves on the burner in your bathroom when Jarvis searched the house."

"Hardly enough to sell on the open market," he answered, then changed the subject abruptly. "I didn't thank you for getting Dan Cassidy down here. He's an excellent lawyer. Without him, I'd be back in custody, at least for the short term."

"Yes, Dan is good. But we're not going to talk about him now. We were talking about this plant and the tea from it that you're making in your bathroom."

He sighed. "It's not illegal—as far as I know, and it's not a drug in the usual sense."

"Andre, stop playing games with me," she cried out in frustration. "I'm tired of all the secrets you're keeping. Just let me in on the punch line."

He brushed his hands on his jeans. "Maybe it's more than you want to know."

"Try me!" Morgan shouted.

Resignation gripped Andre's features. He gestured toward the plants. "I told you about the voodoo curse."

"Yes."

"This is part of it. I have to stay here at Belle Vista. I have to cultivate these plants so I'll have a continual supply of the leaves, because I have to make a tea from them and drink it every day."

"Or what?" Morgan asked.

"Or I'll die," he said in a flat voice. "So if you want to call that being addicted, you can. But I'm the only person I know who needs this stuff. Well, my father and my grandfather did."

She felt her throat clog, but she managed to say, "You've tried to do without it?"

"Yes. For a day and a half. I got very sick. You don't want to hear the details."

"Maybe I do."

He looked up, seeing the gathering shadows, and alarm streaked across his face. "I have to go."

Anger surged inside her. "You always have to go just when the conversation is getting interesting—or maybe I should say dangerous."

"You can think about it any way you want," he muttered, then turned and walked away. "It's getting dark, and I have to leave. Like I told you before, that's not exactly my choice."

"Wait a minute. You can't just say something like that and disappear."

"Watch me."

"Come back here!" she shouted, anger and frustration and fear warring inside her. "You can't walk away from me now."

He ignored her, shouldering his way through the wild rose canes.

As she watched him stride into the bayou, her anger and frustration bubbled up. Scrambling to her feet, she hurried after him, deeper into the swamp, where she'd told herself she didn't want to go.

When he started running, she shouted after him. "You damn coward!"

He didn't bother to answer. Instead he ducked through a tangle of underbrush.

Some part of her knew she should just give up. Why the hell was she pursuing this man, who obviously didn't want anything to do with her? Or maybe she should put it differently. This man who was perfectly comfortable getting into a big e-mail correspondence with a woman who attracted him but whom he couldn't deal with in person—except in bed.

Still, she kept floundering after him, mud splattering up as she crossed a marshy area.

"Go back!" he shouted, running faster through the swamp. She was about to give up when her foot sank through a hole in the ground that hadn't been there moments before. She made a strangled sound as she went down.

Chapter Fifteen

"Morgan!"

She sprawled on the ground, trying to catch her breath, hearing his footsteps reversing their course.

He came down beside her, gathering her to himself, holding her tightly as he looked at her leg and ankle. "Are you okay?"

"I don't know."

He helped her to her feet. "See if you can walk. Put some weight on it."

She did, and the ankle hurt but not too badly.

"Can you make it to the house?" he asked.

She half turned, seeing how far she'd come. "I don't know."

He moved away from her, took a knife out of his pocket and cut a branch, which he stripped down to a smooth pole. "Use this."

"You're not going to help me back inside?"

He looked torn. "I can't."

She had been through so much in the short time she'd been at Belle Vista. Somehow his refusal was the last straw.

"If you go off into the swamp now, I'm leaving tomorrow," she heard herself say.

His face turned stark. "I've been waiting for you to say that all along. If that's the way it has to be, then leave and stop torturing both of us."

She raised her chin. "Me? *I'm* torturing both of us? All you have to do is help me walk—and while you're at it, tell me what the hell is really going on here."

He made a frustrated sound. "I told you, because of the curse, I have to spend the night in the bayou."

"Or what?"

"Stay around here and you'll find out," he said and took a step back.

She tangled her fingers in his shirt. "Andre, please trust me. Start by telling how you got out of the handcuffs."

Pain suffused his features. "If you're still here in the morning, I'll tell you everything." Then he detached her fingers from his shirt and walked into the gathering dark.

For long moments she stared at the spot where Andre had disappeared into the darkness. Then she realized that she could be in serious trouble. Her heart in her throat, she looked back the way she'd come and was relieved to see the lights of the house shining in the darkness. Still, she had to cross uneven ground to get to safety.

Leaning heavily on the pole Andre had cut for her, she started toward the lights.

She wanted to turn her brain off, but thoughts kept whirling around inside her head like spiny little creatures, the spines stabbing at her.

Alone in the darkness, she considered her own life. For two years she had thought that no other man besides Trevor Kirkland would ever matter to her. Then Andre Gascon had started corresponding with her, and everything had begun to change.

It was as though he'd woken her from an emotional

sleep. When he'd taken her in his arms, she'd come instantly alive. He'd made her care about him, even before they met. Even when she'd tried to keep the barriers intact around her heart, he'd broken through.

Yet were her feelings for Andre really hers? Or were her emotions all twisted up with those of another woman—Linette Sonnier? Linette had risked everything when she'd let herself fall in love with a man named Andre Gascon. She'd gone off with him—and lost her life.

Morgan would have liked to think that Linette had nothing to do with her. But somehow the dead woman had reached out across the years and dragged Morgan into her life. That was why her feelings for this Andre were so intense, she told herself.

She reached the edge of the garden, then made her way slowly across the lawn.

Janet was standing rigidly on the back balcony staring into the darkness. When she spotted Morgan, she ran down the steps toward her.

"Are you all right, child?" she gasped.

"I hurt my ankle, but it's not too bad."

"You need ice."

"Yes."

"Can I help you walk?"

"I'm fine."

Janet kept pace beside her. "Did you talk to him?" she finally asked in a strained voice.

"Some."

"What did he say?"

"He's afraid to tell me the truth."

"Because it's hard to talk about it."

"What's your stake in this?" Morgan demanded.

The woman answered at once. "I love him like a son. I want to see him happy."

"Well, he'll have to be happy by himself!" Morgan muttered as she pulled herself carefully up the steps.

"You're leaving?" the housekeeper asked.

"Yes."

Janet made a distressed noise. "I was so sure..." She swallowed, then said, "You can't just walk away from him."

"I think I have to."

"You'll feel better when you have some dinner in you," Janet said hopefully.

Apparently, food was Janet's solution to every problem. But the thought of eating anything now made Morgan's stomach knot. "I'm not hungry. Just fix me a bag with some ice."

The older woman sighed. "All right."

Morgan took the ice pack up to her room and wrapped it in a towel. Sitting in the chair, she propped her leg on the footstool and draped the ice over her ankle. The cold felt wonderful.

When she looked up, Janet was standing there.

"What?"

The woman shuffled her feet. "I came to live here a long time ago."

"I gathered that."

"Yvonne and I are cousins."

"What?" Morgan gasped. This time the question came out high-pitched and surprised.

"I guess you can say I started out as a spy for my family. They urged me to apply for a job at Belle Vista. At first I told them what was going on around the house. I never did care much for the old man. I could see why his wife left him. He was harsh and angry. He thought he'd gotten a raw deal in life. He couldn't be bothered to pay attention to his son. That little boy needed somebody to care about him. And that person turned out to be me. I stayed on. It was easy to love him, easy to help him grow and thrive. My family feels like I switched sides." She sighed. "Maybe you could call it that. I call it giving him a chance."

"And you want me to give him a chance, too?" Morgan asked.

"Yes."

"That would be easier if he'd meet me halfway."

"He's trying, but he's been in a difficult situation for a long time. There was nobody he could trust except me. He's had to rely on himself."

They stared at each other for long moments. Then the housekeeper turned and left.

Morgan sat with the ice pack on her ankle, thinking about what she'd just learned and wondering if it made any difference.

After twenty minutes, she took a quick shower, then dressed in a T-shirt and sweatpants and returned to the chair and the ice pack.

When she looked across at the bed, her chest tightened. She and Andre had made love there. And it had been wonderful, if she dared to be honest. But maybe that was because it had been so long since she'd been in a man's arms. Besides, great sex wasn't enough for a great relationship, she told herself. He had to trust her—in person, not just long-distance. He had to share his fears and his joys with her.

Maybe she would just sit here all night. Early in the morning she was going to pack and leave and go back to her life in Baltimore. She and Andre could start corresponding again. She couldn't hold back a sardonic laugh. Right, they could be pen pals, since that had worked out better than face-to-face lovers.

She forced herself away from the edge of hysteria. Janet had given her some insights, though they didn't make it easier to deal with a man who had so many secrets. Morgan couldn't cope with her own confusion, either. It was almost impossible to judge what she was feeling for Andre when everything was so muddled up.

She might not have planned to go to bed, but she was too exhausted to stay awake. Her head lolled against the chair back, and she slept. Sometime in the early hours of the morning the sound of chanting and drumming woke her. The voodoo priestess was out there again.

It was impossible to ignore the performance. Cautiously Morgan stood, relieved that the ankle felt much better than it had a few hours ago. Walking to the window, she peered out into the darkness.

She told herself that the woman couldn't hurt her. Still, she felt her heart pounding. The reaction made her angry at herself.

Ever since she'd come here, outside forces had been manipulating her. It wasn't just the priestess. Linette Sonnier, a woman who had died almost a hundred years ago, was forcing emotions on her. She was dragging the new arrival at Belle Vista into dreams that were none of her business.

"Linette, you're not playing fair with me," she muttered. "And neither are you, Andre. You've been omitting information every time it's not convenient for you to tell something important." She sucked in a breath and let it out. "And we won't leave you out, Janet. You've been in on the fun and games, too, including that last little meaningful conversation."

Suddenly Morgan had had enough. Sitting around and brooding had never been her style. Since her husband's death, she had taken refuge in action. Feeling as if she was finally taking control of something, she charged down the hall.

Janet came out of her room, looking alarmed. "What are you doing?"

"I'm going out."

"But Yvonne—"

"Yeah, right. How could you miss her?" As she spoke, she kept moving toward the stairs.

"Stay away from her," Janet warned. "Her magic is strong."

"So is mine, and I'm tired of everybody telling me to stay in the house at night," she said over her shoulder as she hurried down the staircase. Before she could change her mind, she stepped out the back door.

The night had been dark as black velvet. But Janet must have switched on the exterior lights, because suddenly the gardens around the house were flooded with yellow illumination.

Still, the priestess was beyond their range. Morgan descended to ground level and walked away from the house, into the darkness—toward the woman who wanted her out of the picture.

That concept rattled around in the back of her head. The priestess *wanted* her to flee this place. So, leaving in the morning would hand her a victory.

Morgan had little time to examine that logic as she zeroed in on the dark shadow under the trees.

Yvonne Sonnier had stopped chanting. She stood silent and still, facing the enemy squarely. Morgan had never seen her up close. She was a small woman with long, dark hair and sharp features, dressed in a simple dark shift.

"You frightened me when I came to town," Morgan said, hearing her voice ring out in the night. "Then you did things to my mind—where the road flooded and at the cemetery. But I've faced enemies a lot stronger than you and I've finally got my head screwed on straight— at least where you're concerned. You can't hurt me anymore."

The words were brave. She hoped they were true as she marched across the lawn, not even sure what would happen.

"Go back inside," the priestess shouted at her. "Go back before you get hurt."

"Make me," Morgan challenged.

Yvonne began to chant again.

Morgan felt her vision suddenly blur and her breath solidify in her lungs. All at once, it was hard to see, hard to breathe. Fear beat against her, but she kept going, determined to fight this woman on her own terms.

She knew she had made headway when the chanting stopped abruptly and the pressure on her lungs eased.

Maybe the deciding factor was that her anger was stronger than her fear.

"Leave Andre Gascon alone," she shouted.

"He's evil."

"No, he isn't. His grandfather loved Linette and she loved him. Tragedy separated them, but that has nothing to do with the man who lives here now."

"She died because of his ancestor."

"No. She died because she wanted a life with him. He didn't coerce her."

"Go away from here, or I'll hurt you."

"Why—because you know Linette spoke to me?"

The woman gasped. "No. You're lying."

"She pulled me into the past. She made me feel her joy with Andre and her pain when she lost her life."

"No!"

"I was with her when the flood took her. I think she wants me here. She wants me to set things right finally. Your grandmother may have cursed Andre's grandfather. But it's time for the hate to end. It's time for love to take over," she said, not even sure what she meant.

The woman looked stunned as Morgan kept advancing. She had no idea what would happen now. Were they going to get into a fight?

It wasn't a human voice that spoke next. From out of the darkness, a roar split the night, and the jaguar leaped forward. Morgan gasped in shock. She'd been so focused on the priestess that she'd forgotten all about the animal that prowled the bayou.

The jaguar gave her a long look, then with a roar in its throat, it turned away and charged Yvonne. Almost instantly it staggered, choking, then toppled onto the ground.

The animal picked itself up, swaying on unsteady legs, then leaped again. Once more it staggered, then fell to the ground, gasping.

Finally it caught its breath, growling in anguish and frustration.

But Morgan wasn't affected by whatever spell Yvonne had worked. Grimly, she ran forward.

The priestess shrieked, and suddenly a knife was in her hand. "Leave me alone!"

"What, you don't trust your magic to kill me?" Morgan shouted, lashing out with her foot.

The woman jumped back, then slashed with the knife. This time Morgan landed a kick on the hand with the weapon. The blade slid along her shoe, then dropped to the ground.

Too angry to think straight, Morgan picked it up and threw it in the direction of the house. With a cry that contained as much fear as anger, the woman turned and ran into the dark night. Morgan picked up the drum and hurled the instrument after her, seeing it hit her back with a satisfying thwack.

She might have pursued the woman, but a deep growl from the jaguar made her whirl around.

She and the animal stood confronting each other for the fourth time. The first had been on the road when the men had attacked her. Next time the animal had been outside the house. Yesterday he had rescued her from Dwight Rivers. Now he was back, when she'd been in trouble again. Only, some major spell had kept him from attacking Yvonne.

She should be afraid of him. He was large and strong, with dangerous claws and teeth. Yet she stood her ground, looking into the fierce yellow eyes.

"Well, here you are, coming to my rescue again. I didn't thank you for the last time," she said. "I mean when Dwight Rivers attacked me."

She didn't expect the animal to speak or even acknowledge the thanks, but he moved his large head in a motion that looked like a nod. She felt as though she were on the verge of an important discovery—and at the same time as though the world was teetering under her feet.

Before anything more could happen, the cat took a step toward the safety of the bayou, then another.

"Wait!" she called out, as she had called out to Andre a few hours earlier. But the beast ignored her as surely as the man had done, and she was left standing alone in the garden with the first hint of dawn teasing the edge of the eastern sky.

Her heart was racing. She wanted to scream in frustration. Every time she felt she was on the edge of finding out what was really happening here, she ran out of time, or people walked away from her.

As she stood clenching and unclenching her fists, a rustling in the underbrush made her stiffen.

Was the cat coming back?

No. It was a man she saw. Andre, barefoot, wearing the shirt and jeans he'd had on the night before.

He stopped a few feet from her, his expression sad and uncertain, but determined.

"What are you hiding this time?" she asked.

"I'm done with hiding anything," he said in a weary voice.

"Is that your trained jaguar?" she tossed at him. "Did you turn down an oil deal so your cat would have space to roam the bayou?"

He gave a mirthless laugh. "I wish it were that simple." He swallowed convulsively. "I told you I was cursed. I told you I have to go out into the bayou every night. I told you I have to drink an extract from that plant to keep myself alive. But there's more to the curse." He looked like a man jumping off a cliff when he said, "The curse turns me into a jaguar every night. That cat isn't my trained pet. I'm the cat."

"No," she answered automatically.

"Yeah, it's hard to believe," he conceded. "Yvonne's grandmother cursed my grandfather—the man who let Linette get swept away in the flood. The people who settled this area believed in voodoo magic. They figured something strange was going on out here. Still, he was a rich man, and my grandmother was willing to marry him for his money, but she didn't stay long after my father was born."

Morgan opened her mouth, but he waved his hand in front of her face. "Let me finish while I have the guts to tell you all of it. The curse fell on my father. He had to stay here and drink the plant extract, but he didn't get the jaguar part. I hoped and prayed that portion of the curse was lifted, but I guess it only skips a generation. When I turned eighteen, I found out I was back where the original Andre Gascon had started."

She fought to catch her breath. "You expect me to believe that?"

"I'm sure you don't want to."

"But you said the…the cat part is at night," she challenged. "I saw the cat twice during the day."

His face softened. "Yes. When the need is great, I can change during the day. I rescued Janet from a bear in the backcountry once. And it was me out on the road after those men made you end up in that ditch. I know you had a gun and you pointed it at the jaguar. That was the first time during the day. The second time was when Dwight Rivers attacked you. The cat leaped over to the island and got him off you. Then Jarvis was coming, and you told the cat to go." He dragged in a breath and huffed it out. "I notice you didn't tell the sheriff anything about the jaguar. Why not? Because you suspected something strange, but you couldn't put it into words?"

"I don't know," she whispered.

"Well, now you know what I've been hiding from you," he said in a barely audible voice. "And you can understand why I didn't want to tell you."

He had given her reason to believe him. Although she fought the truth of what he'd said, she still had one more question. "Is there some way to lift the curse?"

"There's supposed to be…" He looked more somber and downcast than ever before as he said, "But it's hopeless."

Chapter Sixteen

Unable to draw a full breath, Andre kept his gaze fixed on Morgan as he waited for the next logical question.

"Tell me how," she said.

His mouth was so dry that he had to moisten his lips before he could speak. "The priestess said that the spell would be broken if a woman who knew the full extent of the curse came willingly to Andre and gave him her love."

He saw her features contort.

"I knew that was too much to ask of any woman," he said. "I thought I would live out my life alone here, then the murders started, and I knew someone was trying to make me leave. I knew I needed help, so I started checking out detective agencies—and rejecting them. When I saw your name on the Light Street Web site, I knew—" He stopped and ran a hand through his dark hair. "I knew there was something about you that made it seem right. But now I realize I was just fooling myself." He wanted to turn and escape from her, but there was more he had to say before she left. "Thank you for saving me from Dwight Rivers's nasty little plan. You did a fantastic job of detective work. I'll mail your check to Baltimore."

It was finished. Whatever had sprouted between them as they'd typed messages back and forth between Baltimore and Belle Vista had died before the roots could take hold. Defeated, he felt his shoulders slump. Before he could make the confrontation any worse for either of them, he turned and walked away, into the backcountry that he knew so well because he'd roamed these acres every night for the past twelve years.

He stared at the graceful branches of a tupelo tree as he walked away, feeling dead inside. He had bet everything on one roll of the dice and lost.

MORGAN WATCHED him leave her, feeling as though a vise were tightening around her heart. He had told her things she couldn't possibly believe. Terrible things.

Yet she had no alternative but to believe—not after everything that had happened since she'd arrived at Belle Vista. She knew she should run in the other direction. Back to Baltimore where she would be safe.

Logic urged her to flee. Still she understood, on some deep instinctive level, that running away would be the worst mistake of her existence. For the past two years she had felt as though her life was a hollow shell.

Now she had the power to make it much worse.

"No," she whispered.

As Andre walked past a stand of graceful blue water irises, she found herself running after him.

Reaching him, she grabbed at one broad shoulder. He went rigid, then whirled to face her.

"Don't walk away from me again," she whispered.

"You want me to stay after what I just told you? Why? Are you caught in Linette's dream?"

"No," she answered, but she knew she sounded uncertain.

"Are you feeling her emotions? Is that it?"

"Partly. And mine, too." She swallowed, then fought to make sense to him—to herself. "Do you believe in reincarnation?" she asked.

"I don't know."

"You said you dreamed of Andre. Dreams where you were him. Where you knew facts that only he could know."

He nodded.

"And Linette came to me, with a kind of reality that was frightening and confusing." She squeezed her eyes closed, then opened them again. "Linette taught me things I didn't know. I loved my husband. I clung to his memory because it was all I had. But there were elements missing from my marriage, gaps I didn't want to admit. We formed a bond because we were in the same profession—the spy profession—and we could share experiences that we couldn't talk about with anyone else. But that was really all we had. When he died, I was left with nothing. I mean, we hadn't made much of a life. We could have settled down, had children, but we didn't do that."

She felt as though she'd made a terrible confession and at the same time as though a weight had been lifted off her shoulders.

Reaching for Andre, she pulled him toward her and held on tight. His arms came up to embrace her, but she knew he was still afraid to believe they could break the curse together.

She pressed her face to his chest, then tipped her head up so she could meet his gaze. "Don't turn away from me—from us. And don't turn away from the chance to right the wrongs of the past," she whispered, then held her breath, waiting for his answer.

His gaze burned into hers. "You have to be sure. For yourself."

"My feelings are as real as Linette's. What about you?"

"I knew from the minute I found you at Light Street that I had to ask you here."

"Then stop fighting us."

"You don't know me well enough to—"

"I think I do. I came down to Louisiana because we had already formed a strong relationship. Then you did your best to push me away. Now I understand why. You were afraid of what would happen to me if I stayed. And you're still fighting…us. Now do us both a favor and stop it."

When he didn't answer, she grabbed his hand and held on. She felt a shudder go through him. Then he began walking, leading her farther into the bayou, to a place where the ground was covered with soft moss and the light was filtered by tree branches.

He brought her under the shelter of the tree. When he turned to face her, his expression was grave. "We can settle things here. Or you're free to leave," he said.

"Why are you still trying to push me away?"

"I'm giving you time to think rationally," he said in a gritty voice.

"Well, I've always been better at action than thinking."

Her hands weren't quite steady as she reached for the hem of her shirt, pulled it over her head and tossed it on the ground. Then she kicked off her shoes before reaching for the waistband of her sweatpants and skimming them down her legs.

Wearing only her bra and panties, she smiled as she took in the stunned expression on his face. Because she was enjoying herself now, she reached around behind her back and unhooked the bra.

She felt her breath catch as his gaze swept over her. Then he finally spoke, and she thought everything would be all right. "You are so beautiful, standing there with the sunlight and shadow on you," he breathed.

She smiled at him in triumph and in joy. "We could use some more clothing on the moss to make a nice bed," she said.

Still looking as if he didn't entirely believe they were here together, he pulled off his shirt, then his jeans, tossing them atop her clothing. But then he seemed incapable of moving. Or maybe he was simply incapable of believing that she hadn't run away from him after he had told her the worst.

She pulled her panties off, then walked toward him and grasped the elastic band at the top of his briefs, pulling them off, too. Her touch seemed to release him from a spell.

With an urgent sound deep in his throat, he gathered her to him, his mouth coming down on hers for another hungry kiss.

They swayed together, touching, kissing, sighing, neither of them steady on their feet.

"Maybe we'd better get horizontal," she said against his mouth.

"You mean before we topple over?"

"Yes."

They lowered themselves to the makeshift bed, and

he rolled to his back, bringing her down on top of himself, his hands taking long strokes along her back.

"I can't believe this," he whispered.

"I know. But it's real," she said, adjusting herself so that his erection was nestled in the space at the top of her legs.

He cradled her against his body, then rolled them to the side so that his hands could find her breasts, shaping them to his touch, and she responded with a long sigh of pleasure. Bending, he drew one nipple into his mouth, then lavished his attention on the other.

When he looked up, his features were taut as he winnowed his hand through the back of her hair.

"Do you feel the magic?" he asked.

"Yes," she answered, realizing that it was true. They were caught in a bubble of golden light, the only two people in a magic world.

Tender, possessive feelings welled inside her. Not just from herself. From Linette.

"Do you feel them?" she asked. "Andre and Linette?"

"Yes. But why weren't they with us before in the bedroom?"

"Because they were waiting for me to accept you. All of you," she whispered, knowing it was the truth.

She expected him to look relieved. Instead his features clouded. "You're sure this isn't just for them?"

"Of course I'm sure. This is for us. But they want to be here, too," she answered. "They want to share in what we've found together. Don't ask me how I know all that. I just do."

He nodded gravely, then leaned toward her, raining small kisses over her face, her shoulders, her breasts.

"Andre, please, I need you."

"Not yet, *chère*. Let me have the pleasure of touching you, kissing you."

He didn't give her a chance to argue. He stopped her words with his lips on hers as his hand slid down her body and dipped into her most sensitive flesh.

Her hips moved restlessly as he brought her up to an almost unbearable level of desire. She reached down to clasp his erection with her hand, drawing a sharp exclamation from him.

"Please, now," she begged again. "Do it now. Don't make me wait another hundred years."

"I won't." He gave her a long, lingering kiss, then moved over her, stroking his wonderfully hard shaft against her before cupping her hips, lifting her as he drove forward and into her.

"Andre!" She called his name as he began to move within her, then kept pace with him as he quickened the tempo.

They were Andre and Morgan.

Andre and Linette—the lovers who had waited so long for their fulfillment.

When his hand slipped between them to stroke her, she came undone for him in a soul-shattering explosion of pleasure.

Above her, he cried out, following her over the edge into ecstasy.

She drifted back to earth in his arms, stroking the damp skin of his back and shoulders, then kissing his cheek.

She clung to him for long moments, then said in a strong voice, "It's over. The curse is over."

He didn't answer as he moved to her side. When he tried to shift away from her, she kept him close.

Raising his head, he looked at her. "You're forgetting about Yvonne."

"No, I'm not. She can't hurt us."

"She doesn't fight fair," he murmured.

"She has to now, because loving you gives me the strength to defeat her. I didn't understand that a while ago. I understand it now."

He looked stunned, and she gave him a reassuring smile.

"You can't quite believe you've found a woman who can freely love you. But you will," she said, reaching down to knit her fingers with his. "It's over. Your life is going to change now."

"How do you know it's over?" he asked, his voice grating, and she realized that despite making love with her, he still had trouble changing the way he thought of himself.

She moved her head against his shoulder. "Because love changes everything."

As if in response to her words, something flickered at the edge of her vision. When she looked up, she gasped.

Beside her, Andre stiffened. "What? What's wrong?"

"Over there," she managed, pointing.

He followed the direction of her hand and his breath caught. A jaguar was standing in the swamp, about twenty feet away, staring at them. Well, not a real, solid jaguar, because she could look right through the cat to the foliage on the other side of him.

"You see that?" she asked, unable to raise her voice above a whisper.

"Yes," Andre answered, his tone awed.

The big cat stood regarding them. It swished its tail, then opened its mouth, raised its head and roared. Only there was no sound.

Slowly it turned and began to walk away from them, into the bayou. And the farther it got, the more light she could see shining through the mass of the animal, until there was nothing left of the cat at all.

Beside her, Andre made a strangled sound. "It's gone. I saw it leave. I felt it leave me."

"Yes. The cat that haunted you has vanished."

He stared after the animal, but she knew he still wasn't entirely convinced.

She took him in her arms, hugging him tightly, wanting to hold him forever out here in this beautiful natural setting that he knew so well. But they had other obligations.

"We should go back, so Janet won't worry about us," she said.

He nodded. "I wasn't thinking about her."

"I'm glad you were focused on us." She hesitated for a moment, then said, "But we have to think about her, too. She cares about you very much."

"Yes."

Quietly they both moved off the makeshift bed and began getting dressed.

Andre bent to pluck a piece of greenery from her sweatpants, and she did the same for his shirt. Then, hand in hand, they walked back toward the house.

"So will you tell me how you got out of the hand-cuffs?" she asked.

"I did it when I changed into the cat."

"Oh."

As they reached the lawn, Morgan saw a lone fig-ure was standing on the balcony, staring out toward the swamp.

It was Janet.

When she spotted them, she hurried down the stairs, then stopped short as she gave them an assessing appraisal.

Morgan felt herself flushing as she fought not to look down at the rumpled clothing that had served as bedding not so long ago. Probably she should have checked more carefully for bits of moss and other debris.

A small smile flickered on Janet's lips. "You look like you…worked out your differences," she said in a soft voice.

"Yes," Morgan murmured, then asked the question that had been bothering her since she'd first come here. Looking the housekeeper directly in the eye, she asked, "Did you put that robe in with the items for the church sale?"

Janet shook her head. "I may have. I…don't honestly know."

"Maybe we have to chalk it up to magic. Good magic," Morgan answered.

"Yes," the housekeeper agreed.

"One more question, did you rake away the jaguar prints from a few nights ago?"

This time, the housekeeper looked contrite, then nodded.

"Why?"

"I didn't want you to see them."

"I understand," Morgan murmured.

"Come inside. I made some more of those cinnamon buns," Janet said, changing the subject abruptly, and Morgan decided not to make an issue of anything that had happened over the past few days.

When they walked into the kitchen, they found Dan Cassidy sitting at the table polishing off one of the buns.

Morgan stared at him. "What are you doing here?"

"Checking up on you," he said easily, looking her up and down. "And it seems that I can give Jo a positive report."

"Yes." Because she was feeling a little unsteady on her feet, she dropped into a chair. Andre remained standing.

"So, are you coming back to Baltimore or staying here?" Dan asked.

Her gaze shot to Andre. "We haven't talked about that yet."

"Well, you've worked two solid years without a vacation. I think you've got at least six weeks to decide what you want to do."

Dan looked at Andre. "I think you're good for her. Just stay out of trouble with the law, okay?"

"I'll try my best," he answered.

DAN LEFT after breakfast.

Morgan could see Andre was restless. She knew that he wouldn't feel entirely free of the curse until after dark, so she said she was worn-out, which was true, and went off to take a nap.

When she woke, she found she'd slept away most of the day. Looking out the window, she saw Andre working in the garden. His refuge.

After taking a shower, she put on a sundress and sandals and a little makeup before going down to consult Janet. Then she made a phone call.

Andre stopped working as she approached him, eyeing the sun, which was now low in the western sky.

"I made us dinner reservations in town," she said.

His features immediately clouded. "I never eat in town."

"Well, I'd like to try it tonight. Why don't you go shower and change."

He hesitated for a moment, still looking uncomfortable. Then, his expression became resigned. "All right," he said in a low voice.

"We should leave in about forty minutes," she told him.

But as she waited on the sun porch, she felt her own tension mounting.

Andre stepped onto the porch at the appointed time, looking wonderful in a white button-down shirt and dark slacks. But she saw that he wasn't exactly relaxed.

"Let's go. If you like, I can drive," she said.

He nodded, but he looked as if he wanted to back out.

She had timed their departure carefully. The sun was a red ball of flame just above the trees as they headed toward St. Germaine. Andre sat with his hands clasped tightly in his lap, the knuckles white. He kept glancing at the door as though he was ready to leap out of the car if he had to.

She wanted to reach out and cover his hands with hers. She wanted to tell him that everything had changed. But she suspected he wouldn't believe her yet, so she simply kept driving.

As the sun disappeared, he shuddered, his face rigid, his eyes focused on the windshield.

As twilight descended over the bayou, she heard him make a strangled sound. When she turned to him, she saw tears trickling down his cheeks.

She pulled to the shoulder, slammed the car into park and reached for him. He came into her arms, and she held him, feeling his shoulders shake.

"I couldn't…I didn't…"

"I know. I know," she murmured as she held him, stroking his back, combing her fingers through his dark hair. "You couldn't believe it until dark. But it's all over now. It's really all over."

He fumbled in his pocket for a handkerchief and blew his nose. "I'm acting like a child."

"No. You're just being emotional. I'm glad that you can be. You were so rigid, so controlled."

"I had to be."

"I know."

He clasped her tightly, kissed her.

She drove the rest of the way into town, slowing as she passed Yvonne's house. The lights were off and the curtains were closed.

"She's in there," Andre muttered.

"Or she's not. It doesn't matter to us," she said, knowing that was another truth he'd have to learn to accept.

Her next stop was the gas station, where the same group of guys were sitting on the bench out front. Pulling up next to the pump, she said to Andre, "Why don't you top off the tank."

"I'd be glad to," he answered in a steady voice, getting out. .

She kept her eyes on the men, then grinned as she saw them react to the presence of Andre Gascon in their midst, after dark.

Bubba came rushing over, then stopped short, watching Andre fill the tank.

"You've never been here at night," he said, sounding like he expected a jaguar to materialize in front of him.

Andre shrugged as he deliberately continued pumping gas, then got out his wallet to pay. He looked calm, as if this was just a routine trip into town. But she knew how much the moment meant to him.

He was grinning as he climbed back into the car.

"I guess that was fun," she murmured.

"Like dropping water bombs out of the second-floor window at school."

"Did you ever do that?"

"I was too well behaved."

"Well, I did it. And got in big trouble," she admitted.

"I'll bet."

She drove to one of the restaurants on Main Street, a charming Cajun bistro that Janet had recommended.

Again they drew stares as they entered and walked out back to a quiet table on the patio.

They ordered champagne, and when the waitress had left them alone again, Andre raised his glass. "There's so much I want to say," he said, emotion thickening his voice.

"Just tell me you can accept being happy," she whispered.

"I can. Well, I hope I can."

They touched glasses, then each took a sip.

When he shifted in his seat, she reached for his hand and squeezed it. "What?"

"You have good friends back in Baltimore."

"Yes. But I'd like to stay here—if you want me to," she added, because they hadn't talked about the future.

His hand tightened on hers. "I love you. I want you for my wife, if you'll have me."

"Oh, yes."

He sighed. "Another hurdle crossed."

"But I think I'll have to let Janet run the house."

"Would you mind?" he asked.

"Actually, I never much liked housekeeping. I think I can get used to someone who keeps the place spotless and the kitchen full of great food."

"Good."

She cleared her throat. "But sitting around doing nothing would be impossible. I'll need a job. What would you think about my running for sheriff?"

"Not a bad idea."

"With some time off for maternity leave," she said softly.

"I thought I would never have a wife. Never have a family," he whispered.

"But you like the idea of children?"

"Your children," he said, as if he still couldn't quite believe the discussion was real.

Their food came, and she realized she hadn't paid much attention to what she had ordered. She'd come here to make a statement. Now she wanted to get back home—back to Belle Vista.

Both of them ate a little of the meal.

"We should talk about the oil reserves," he finally said. "I guess it's not fair to withhold them from the market when the country needs oil."

"I agree with that. But it's up to you."

"I'm hoping I can find consultants who can help us minimize any damage to the natural environment."

"Yes."

They went back to the food, but both of them finished only about half the meal.

"You're not hungry?" Andre asked.

She grinned at him. "I think we'd both rather be home in bed."

He grinned back, and she loved the way it changed

his looks. Probably it would take him a while to realize that the terrible tension had gone out of his life. But
she was going to be beside him, helping him every step
of the way.

When they climbed back into the car, she started to
turn the key in the ignition, but he put his hand on her
arm.

"One more thing," he said in a thick voice. Reaching into his pocket, he pulled out something that glinted
in the floodlights from the restaurant.

When she saw the gold locket in his hand, she
gasped. "Where did you get that?"

"I found it in the bayou." He clicked it open, and she
stared down at the portraits. They had been damaged a
little by the water. But when she studied the features of
the man and woman, she gasped again.

"They look like us."

"Yes."

"You had this before I came?"

"Yes. But I wasn't going to show it to you
until…unless…"

"I understand," she whispered.

His hands were shaking as he lifted the locket from
her fingers and clasped it around her neck.

As it settled against her chest, she sighed. "Thank
you for bringing me back here."

"You feel like this is home?" he asked, sounding
stunned.

"Oh, yes. Always and forever, with you."

Like a phantom in the night
comes an exciting promotion from

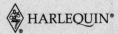
HARLEQUIN®

INTRIGUE®

ECLIPSE

GOTHIC ROMANCE

Look for a provocative
gothic-themed thriller each month
by your favorite Intrigue authors!
Once you surrender to the classic
blend of chilling suspense and
electrifying romance in these
gripping page-turners, there will
be no turning back....

Available wherever Harlequin books are sold.

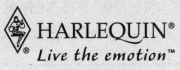
HARLEQUIN®
Live the emotion™

www.eHarlequin.com   HIE3

ATHENA FORCE

The Athena Academy adventure continues....

Three secret sisters
Three super talents
One unthinkable legacy...

The ties that bind may be the ties that kill as these extraordinary women race against time to beat the genetic time bomb that is their birthright....

**Don't miss the latest three stories
in the Athena Force continuity**

DECEIVED by Carla Cassidy, January 2005

CONTACT by Evelyn Vaughn, February 2005

PAYBACK by Harper Allen, March 2005

**And coming in April–June 2005,
the final showdown for
Athena Academy's best and brightest!**

Available at your favorite retail outlet.

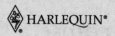
HARLEQUIN®

INTRIGUE®

Opens the case files on:

TOP SECRET BABIES

Unwrap the mystery!

January 2005
UNDERCOVER BABIES
by ALICE SHARPE

February 2005
MOMMY UNDER COVER
by DELORES FOSSEN

March 2005
NOT-SO-SECRET BABY
by JO LEIGH

April 2005
PATERNITY UNKNOWN
by JEAN BARRETT

Follow the clues to your favorite retail outlet!

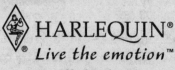

HARLEQUIN®
Live the emotion™

www.eHarlequin.com

HITSB2

If you enjoyed what you just read,
then we've got an offer you can't resist!

Take 2 bestselling love stories FREE!

Plus get a FREE surprise gift!

Clip this page and mail it to Harlequin Reader Service®

IN U.S.A.	IN CANADA
3010 Walden Ave.	P.O. Box 609
P.O. Box 1867	Fort Erie, Ontario
Buffalo, N.Y. 14240-1867	L2A 5X3

YES! Please send me 2 free Harlequin Intrigue® novels and my free surprise gift. After receiving them, if I don't wish to receive anymore, I can return the shipping statement marked cancel. If I don't cancel, I will receive 4 brand-new novels each month, before they're available in stores! In the U.S.A., bill me at the bargain price of $4.24 plus 25¢ shipping and handling per book and applicable sales tax, if any*. In Canada, bill me at the bargain price of $4.99 plus 25¢ shipping and handling per book and applicable taxes**. That's the complete price and a savings of at least 10% off the cover prices—what a great deal! I understand that accepting the 2 free books and gift places me under no obligation ever to buy any books. I can always return a shipment and cancel at any time. Even if I never buy another book from Harlequin, the 2 free books and gift are mine to keep forever.

181 HDN DZ7N
381 HDN DZ7P

Name	(PLEASE PRINT)	
Address	Apt.#	
City	State/Prov.	Zip/Postal Code

Not valid to current Harlequin Intrigue® subscribers.

Want to try two free books from another series?
Call 1-800-873-8635 or visit www.morefreebooks.com.

* Terms and prices subject to change without notice. Sales tax applicable in N.Y.
** Canadian residents will be charged applicable provincial taxes and GST.
  All orders subject to approval. Offer limited to one per household.
  ® are registered trademarks owned and used by the trademark owner and or its licensee.

INT04R   ©2004 Harlequin Enterprises Limited

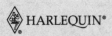

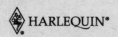